THE MING VASE

Inside Cartwright House, a secret Government military project takes place. Men and women are well cared for, with every leisure facility. But they are prisoners, forbidden to leave. Their defection to, or capture by, foreign powers could be catastrophic. These people have very special powers, capable of being harnessed by enemies who could threaten and destroy western civilization. So when Klieger does escape, Special C.I.A. agent Don Gregson must find him. The only clue? Klieger has stolen a Ming Vase.

E. C. TUBB

THE MING VASE

Complete and Unabridged

LINFORD
Leicester

First published in Great Britain

First Linford Edition
published 2012

British Library CIP Data

Tubb, E. C.
  The Ming vase. - - (Linford mystery library)
  1. Suspense fiction.
  2. Large type books.
  I. Title II. Series
  823.9'14–dc23

  ISBN 978–1–4448–1222–0

Published by
F. A. Thorpe (Publishing)
Anstey, Leicestershire

Set by Words & Graphics Ltd.
Anstey, Leicestershire
Printed and bound in Great Britain by
T. J. International Ltd., Padstow, Cornwall

This book is printed on acid-free paper

THE MING VASE

The antique shop was one of those high-class places, which catered only to the very rich and the very possessive. A single vase of hand-worked glass stood in one window, an Egyptian Solar Boat in the other, between them the door presented a single expanse of unbroken glass to the street outside.

Don Gregson paused before it, deep-set eyes curious as he stared at the street. There was no trace of the accident. The wreckage had been removed and the rain had washed away the last traces of blood. Even the inevitable sightseers had gone about their business. Turning back to the door he pushed it open and stepped into the warmth inside.

Earlman was there, and Bronson, both standing beside a small, elderly man with delicate hands and intelligent eyes. Some assistants hovered discreetly in the background. The police had left and Don was glad of it. Earlman stepped forward.

'Hi, Don. You made good time.'

'The general sees to that. Is that the owner?'

Max nodded, gesturing to the little man. Quickly he made the introductions.

'Mr. Levkin this is Don Gregson, C.I.A., Special Department.'

They shook hands. Don was surprised at the wiry strength in the delicate fingers. Bronson, as usual, merely stood and watched; a coiled spring waiting his moment of release.

'I wish we could have met under happier circumstances,' said Don to the owner. 'Please tell me all about it.'

'Again?'

'If you please. First-hand reports are always the most reliable.'

Levkin shrugged and spread his hands in a gesture almost as old as time.

'I have been robbed,' he said with simple understatement. 'I have been robbed of the most precious item in my shop. It was small, a vase from the Ming Dynasty, but it was beautiful. You understand?'

'How small?'

Levkin gestured with his hands and Don nodded.

'About six inches high, small enough to slip into a pocket. You said that it was valuable. How valuable?'

'I said that it was precious,' corrected the owner. 'How do you value a work of art? The price is what the purchaser is prepared to pay. Let me say only that I have refused five hundred thousand dollars for it.'

Earlman grunted, his thin, harassed face and dark, bruised-looking eyes veiled behind the smoke of his cigarette.

'Tell us about the man.'

'He was medium built, medium height, well-dressed, brown hair and eyes . . . remarkable eyes. About a hundred and seventy pounds, softly spoken, very gentle and polite.'

Over Levkin's head Earlman caught Don's eye and nodded.

'Nothing ostentatious,' continued Levkin. 'Nothing which gave a hint that he was not what he seemed. I had no reason to suspect that he was a thief.'

'He isn't,' said Don, then frowned at

his own absurdity. 'Go on.'

'We spoke. He was interested in rare and beautiful things; it was natural that I should show him the vase. Then there was a crash in the street, an accident. Inevitably we turned and headed towards the door. It was a bad accident, our attention was distracted, but only for a moment. It was enough. By the time I remembered the man had gone and he had taken the vase with him.'

'Are you positive as to that?' Don laboured the point. 'Could it be hidden here somewhere? Anywhere?'

'The police asked that. No, it is not hidden. I have made a thorough search. It has been stolen.' For the first time the man displayed emotion. 'Please, you will get it back? You will do your best?'

Don nodded, jerking his head at Earlman as he stepped to one side. Bronson, as always, joined them.

'How about the identification?' Don spoke in a trained whisper inaudible two feet from his lips. 'Is it positive?'

'They swear to the photograph. It's our man all right.'

'I've got to be certain. How about the accident? Could that have been faked?'

'Not a chance. A cab hit a pedestrian and swerved into a truck. The jaywalker's dead, the cabbie will lose a leg and the truck driver's in a bad way. That was no rigged diversion.'

'Coincidence?' Don shook his head. 'No, the timing was too limited for that. Levkin's no fool and even the smartest crook requires a certain reaction time before he can spot an opportunity, weigh his chances and then swing into action. Levkin would never have given an ordinary crook that much time. It looks as if you're right, Max.'

'I am right. It was Klieger.' Earlman looked puzzled. 'But why, Don? Why?'

Gregson didn't answer. His face was strained, thoughtful.

'Why?' repeated Earlman. 'Why should he want to steal a thing he can't sell, can't eat, can't do anything with but sit and look at? Why?'

★ ★ ★

General Penn asked the same question, but unlike Earlman he demanded an answer. Slumped in his chair behind the wide desk he looked even older and more harassed than he had when this whole thing had started. Don could understand that. The general, literally, had his neck on the block.

'Well?' The voice reflected the strain. Harsh, heavy with irritating undertones, it carried too much of a barrack square, too little of understanding or patience. 'You've found what you said to look for. Now, what's the answer?'

'We've found something I said might possibly happen,' corrected Don. 'It has. What answer are you looking for?'

'Are you crazy?' Penn surged out of his chair. 'You know what the top-priority is! Find Klieger! What other answer would I be interested in?'

'You might,' said Don quietly, 'be interested in finding out just why he left in the first place.'

Penn said a word. He repeated it. Don tensed then forced himself to relax. Slowly he lit a cigarette.

'Three weeks ago,' he said, 'Albert Klieger decided to leave Cartwright House and did so. Since then you've had all field units concentrate on the one object of finding him. Why?'

'Because he is the greatest potential danger to this country walking on two legs!' Penn spat the words as if they were bullets. 'If he gets to the other side and spills what he knows, we'll lose our greatest advantage in the cold war and the hot war when it comes. Gregson, you know all this!'

'I've been told it,' said Don. He didn't look at the congested face of the general. 'And if we find him and he doesn't want to return, what then?'

'We'll worry about that when we've found him,' said Penn grimly. Don nodded.

'Is that why Bronson is always with my team? Why other men just like him accompany all field units?' He didn't press for an answer. 'Have you ever wondered why the English stopped using the Press Gang system? They knew it wasn't humane from the beginning but, for a while, it worked — for a while and up to a point. Maybe we could learn something from that if we tried.'

'You talk like a fool.' Penn slumped back into his chair. 'No one press-ganged Klieger. I found him in a third-rate carnival and gave him the chance to help his country. He took that chance. It's fair to say that we've given him far more than he's given us. After all, Klieger isn't the only one.'

'That,' said Don, 'is the whole point.' He stared directly at the general. 'How long is it going to be before others in the Project . . . sorry, Cartwright House, decide that they've had enough?'

'There'll be no more walking out.' Penn was very positive. 'I've tripled the security guards and installed gimmicks which makes that impossible.'

It was, of course, a matter of locking the stable door after the horse had been stolen, but Don didn't point that out. Penn, with his reputation and career in the balance, could only be pushed so far at a time. And, to Penn, his career was all-important. Not even Cartwright House came before that.

Which, thought Don bitterly, was the inevitable result of a military machine based on political manoeuvrings. What a man was, what he could do, that was unimportant against who he knew, what he could do for others. Don himself had no illusions. He was useful but he could be branded, damned, kicked out and made the scapegoat if Penn felt he needed a sacrifice. And time was running out.

'We've got to find him.' Penn drummed on the desk. 'Gregson, why can't you find him?'

'You know why. I've trailed him and found where he's been a dozen times. But always too late. To catch him I've got to be where he is when he is, or before he gets there. And that's impossible.'

'This theft.' Penn's mind veered to the latest scrap of information. 'Money I can understand, but why a Ming vase? The guy must be crazy.'

'He isn't normal, but he isn't crazy.' Don crushed out his cigarette. 'And I've an idea that he has a very good reason for wanting that vase. The chances are that

11

he will be collecting other, similar things, how many depends on circumstances.'

'But why?'

'They're beautiful. To those that appreciate them such objects are beyond price. Klieger must have an intensely artistic streak. He has a reason for wanting to own them and it worries me.'

Penn snorted.

'I need more information.' Don was decisive. 'Without it I'm fighting a shadow. I've got to go where I can get it.'

'But — '

'I've got to. There's no other way. None in the world.'

★ ★ ★

No one called it a prison. No one even called it a Project because everyone knew that a 'Project' was both military and important. So it was called Cartwright House and it was a little harder to get into than Fort Knox and far more difficult to leave than Alcatraz.

Don waited patiently as his identification was checked, double-checked, cleared to a higher level and then checked again. It took time but finally he faced Leon Malchin, tall, thin, burning with frustrated zeal and with the courtesy rank of colonel, which meant nothing until he tried to act like a civilian when he felt the full impact of military discipline.

'General Penn has contacted me,' he said. 'I am to offer you every assistance.' He stared at Don through old-fashioned spectacles. 'How can I help you?'

'Question,' said Don. 'How do normal men catch a clairvoyant?'

'You mean Klieger, of course?'

'Of course.'

'They can't. They don't.' Malchin settled back in his chair, a glint of amusement in his eyes. 'Next question?'

'There is no next question — not yet.' Don took the other chair and proffered his cigarettes. Malchin shook his head and sucked at a brier.

'I am a hunter,' said Don abruptly. 'I hunt men. I'm good at it because I have a knack, talent, skill — you name it — for being able to outguess my quarry. You might say that I have a series of lucky hunches. Somehow, I don't know how, I *know* what they will do next — where they will be and when. I have never yet failed to get my man.'

'But you haven't got Klieger.' Malchin nodded as if he had expected this visit for some time. 'And you want to know why.'

'I know why. He is a clairvoyant. What I want to know is how. How does he do it? How does he operate? How effective is he?'

'Very effective.' Malchin took his pipe from his mouth and stared into the bowl. 'He is, or was, our star resident. He could see further than anyone I have ever investigated — and I have invested psi phenomena all my adult life.'

'Go on.'

'I don't think you fully realize just what you are up against in Klieger. He isn't a superman, of course; nothing like that, but he has this one talent. You are, in a sense, a blind man trying to trap a man who can see. Trap him in broad daylight on an open plain. You are also wearing a bell around your neck to attract his attention. Personally I do not think you

14

have a ghost of a chance.'

'How,' Don insisted, 'does this talent work?'

'I don't know.' Malchin anticipated the next question. 'You don't mean that, of course, what you mean is how does he use it. If I knew how it worked I would be a very happy man.' He frowned, searching for words. 'This is going to be difficult to describe. How could you explain sight to a man born blind, or sound to a man born deaf? And you, at least, could tell how these senses 'worked'. However — '

Don lit another cigarette, listening to Malchin's explanations, building pictures in his mind. A piece of rough fabric, each thread of which was a person's life stretching into the future. Some threads were short, others longer, all meshed and interwoven so that it was almost impossible to follow any single thread. But, with training and skill it could be done. Then events came clear and action could be planned.

A bank where a teller suffered an attack of acute appendicitis just as he was counting out a sheaf of notes — and a man who calmly picked them up as if he had just cashed a cheque.

A store where the takings were left unattended for just that essential few minutes of time.

A penthouse apartment and an officer who sneezed just as the quarry walked past.

An antique shop and an accident to create the necessary diversion.

So simple when you could see exactly what would happen and exactly how to take advantage of it.

How to catch Klieger?

Don jerked upright as the cigarette burned his fingers and became aware of Malchin's stare.

'I was thinking of your analogy,' he said. 'You know, the blind man trying to trap the one who could see. I know how it can be done.'

'Yes?'

'The blind man gets eyes.'

* * *

They were comfortable. They had soft beds and good food, canned music,

16

television, a library of books and private movies. They had games and a swimming pool and even a bowling alley. They wore good clothes and were fit and looked it, but they were intelligent and they knew.

A prison is somewhere you can't leave when you want to and they were in prison.

For their own protection, naturally. The guards, the gimmicks, the restrictions were solely designed to keep unwanted people out. The secrecy was from fear of spies and patriotism was the excuse for all. But the things designed to keep people out worked just as well to keep others in.

And, sometimes, patriotism as an excuse wears a little thin.

'It's good to see a new face.' Sam Edwards, fifty, built like a boy with the face of a boxer, grinned as he gripped Don's hand. 'You joining the club?'

'He's just visiting.' A wizened oldster sucked at his teeth as he peered at Don from the depths of an easy chair. 'Say, Gregson, if you fancy a little poker later on I guess we could accommodate you.'

He laughed with a wheezy effort then frowned and slammed a hand on his knee.

'Goldarn it! I miss my poker!'

'Telepaths,' whispered Malchin. 'Most of them are in permanent rapport with others who are you-know-where. I won't bother to introduce you around.'

Don nodded, staring uneasily at the assembled 'residents'. Some were old, a few young, most were middle-aged. They watched him with eyes glinting with secret amusement.

'Oddly enough most of them seem to stick together according to their various talents,' mused Malchin. 'You've seen the telepaths, in this room are those with telekinetic abilities. Nothing standing in the way of progress as yet, but they are getting on. In here are the clairvoyants.'

There were fifteen of them. Don was surprised at the number. Then he wondered why he was surprised. In the great cross-section of humanity that was the United States every deviation from the norm must have been repeated many times. Shrewdly he guessed that he saw only a part of the whole; that Cartwright House was duplicated many times under many names.

'We have found,' whispered Malchin, 'that communal use of their talent greatly aids development of that talent. Klieger was little more than a carnival fortune-teller when he joined us; in ten years he became amazingly proficient.'

'Ten years?'

'That's what I said. Many of our residents have been here longer than that.'

If there was irony in Malchin's voice, Don didn't catch it. But one of the men in the room did. He came forward, hand outstretched, a taut smile on his face.

'Tab Welker,' he said. 'Maybe you can settle an argument. In England, from what I hear, a man sentenced to life imprisonment usually gets out in about nine years. Right?'

'It depends on his conduct.' Don felt his skin tighten as he saw what the man was driving at. 'A life term in England is about fifteen years. A third remission would make it about what you say.'

'And that's usually given for nothing short of murder.' Tab nodded. 'You know, I've been here eight years. One more year to go — maybe!'

'You're not a prisoner,' said Don. The man laughed.

'Please.' He lifted his hand. 'No arguments, no speeches!' He lost his smile. 'What do you want?'

'Help,' said Don simply.

He moved about the room, halting by a small table bearing chessmen set on a board. They were of wood lovingly carved with the unfinished look of true hand-production. He lifted a knight and studied it, then met Welker's eyes.

'Klieger's?'

'How did you guess?' Tab's eyes softened as he stared at the chessmen. 'Albert loved beautiful things. The thing he missed most while in here was being able to visit the museums. He always said that man's true achievements were to be found in the things he had made to ornament his life.'

'Things like vases?'

'Paintings, statuary, cameos, he liked

them all providing they were well made.'

'A man with artistic appreciation.' Don nodded. 'I understand. When did you all decide to help him escape?'

'I . . . What did you say?'

'You heard what I said.' Don's eyes locked with those of the other man then, slowly, Welker smiled.

'You're no fool,' he said. Don returned the smile.

'Now I've another question.' He paused, conscious of the men and their watching eyes. 'Just what does Klieger hope to gain?'

        * * *

'No!' General Penn slammed his hand down on the arm of the backseat. 'No! No!'

Don sighed, staring through the windows at the rain. It dripped from the trees above, pinging on the roof of the car, dewing the glass with a glitter of transient pearls. Further down the road the rear of another car loomed vague through the rain. Behind them would be another. Their own driver was somewhere up ahead probably cursing the odd exigencies of the Service.

'Listen,' said the general, 'we've got word that they know about Klieger. Don't ask me how they even guessed he was important to us, but they do. Now it's a race between us. We daren't lose.'

'We won't lose,' said Don. 'But we'll have to do it my way. It's the only way there is.'

'No.'

'General!' Don released his pent-up temper and frustration in a furious blast of sound. 'What other way is there?'

It stopped Penn as he knew it would, but only for a moment.

'I can't risk it,' he snapped. 'Klieger's only one man, dangerous but still only one. We can handle one man, but can we handle a dozen or more? It's treasonable even to suggest it.'

Don fumed as he recognized the emotion-loaded semantic symbol. Penn with his mania for security had probably aroused unwelcome attention in the first place. Like now when he had insisted that they meet in a car on a road in the rain

22

for fear of some undetected electronic ear waiting to catch their conversation. For long moments the silence dragged, then Don drew a deep breath.

'Treasonable or not it's something you have to consider. For one thing the escape was organized. The lights failed — a telepathically controlled rat gnawed a vital cable. A guard was taken sick for no apparent reason and, for a moment, there was a blank spot in the defences. There were other things, all small, not one coincidental. The whole lot could have walked right out.'

'But they didn't!' Penn pounded the arm of the rear seat. 'Only Klieger. That proves something.'

'That he wanted to run to the Reds?' Don shrugged. 'Then what's keeping him? He's had plenty of time to make contact if that's what he wanted.'

'What's your point?' Penn was losing his patience. 'Are you trying to tell me that those . . . freaks back there are holding a gun to my head? They'll help, you say, but on their terms. Terms!' His hand closed into a fist. 'Don't they understand that the country is as good as at war?'

'They want the thing we keep saying we are fighting to protect,' said Don. 'They want a little freedom. Is that such an outrageous demand?'

He leaned back, closing his eyes, seeing again the faces of the men back in Cartwright House. Some of them, so Malchin had said, had been there twelve years. A long time. Too long to be willing guinea pigs so that their talents could be trained and developed and exploited. But to the general they weren't men. They were 'freaks'; just another weapon to be used, to be protected and hidden, to be destroyed if there was a chance they might fall into enemy hands.

'What?' He opened his eyes, conscious that the general was talking to him. Penn glowered and repeated what he had said. 'Can you catch him, even if they won't help you?'

'I don't know.' Don pursed his lips, shadowed eyes introspective beneath prominent brows. 'I feel that we've gone about this thing in the wrong way. We've thought of it as just another manhunt and we've failed because we're trying to catch no ordinary man. There must be a purpose behind what Klieger did. Find the reason for his leaving and we'll find the purpose.'

'Isn't that what you went to find out?' Penn made no effort to hide his sarcasm.

'Yes. I didn't fail.'

'Then — ?'

'He stole a rare vase of the Ming Dynasty,' said Don. 'Find out why and you have the answer.'

* * *

Max Earlman lay supine on the bed and stared at the ceiling. The hotel room was warm, littered with the personal effects of the three men. Against one wall a large-scale map of the city hung slightly out of true, the grid pattern of streets marked with a host of colored pins. Beyond the windows the early evening had softened the harsh outlines of the concrete jungle, turning even the garish illuminations into things of glowing beauty.

Bronson stirred where he sat at a table,

the thin reek of gun oil harsh to Earlman's nostrils. He lit a cigarette to kill the odour and stared distastefully at the other man.

'Do you have to do that?' Smoke plumed from the cigarette as Max gestured towards the pistol Bronson was cleaning. Bronson continued with his business.

'What gives with you, Bronson?' Earlman swung to his feet, nerves taut with irritation. 'You walk and eat and sleep and I guess you can make noises, too, if you put your mind to it, but are you really a man?'

Metal clicked with deadly precision as Bronson reassembled the gun. He tucked it into its holster, drew it with a fantastic turn of speed, and returned it again.

Earlman jerked forward, anger burning in the deep, bruised-looking eyes. He turned as Don entered the room. He looked tired.

'No luck?' Max knew the answer. Don shook his head.

'We're still on our own.' Crossing the room he stood before the map, studying the clusters of coloured pins. 'Have you got them all?'

'Every single one.' Earlman blew smoke

at the map. 'If anyone ever tells me this city has no culture, I'll tear them apart. The place is lousy with art galleries, museums, exhibitions, antique shops, displays, missions and what have you. I've marked them all.' He looked sideways at Gregson's bleak face. 'There are a lot, Don. Too many.'

'We can whittle them down.' Don sighed, feeling the tension of the past few weeks building up inside, the tautness of the past few days stretching his nerves. He forced himself to relax, taking deep breaths, forgetting the urgency and Penn's hysterical demands.

'Cut out foreign films, contemporary art, modernist paintings, exhibitions of abstract design. Eliminate the stamp collections, trade missions, engineering displays. Concentrate on the old, the rare, the beautiful.'

'How close should I go?'

'Close. Keep the unusual, the short-term, the items loaned from private collections.'

Earlman nodded and busied himself with the coloured pins and a sheaf of catalogues. Don turned and stared out of the window.

Below him the city sprawled, scar-like streets slashing between soaring anthills of concrete, the whole glittering with light. Somewhere in the city another man probably stood staring from a window — a mild man with a love of artistic things. A man who, until recently, had lived a law-abiding existence and who, suddenly, had broken the conditioning of a lifetime to rob and steal and run.

Why?

Frustration, yes, all the 'residents' of Cartwright House were frustrated, but they had remained when they could have fled. Only Klieger had run and had kept running. Now he was somewhere in the city, his talent warning him of approaching danger, showing him how to dodge and move and avoid so as to remain free.

Free in order to do what?

Don sighed, wondering for the thousandth time just how it must feel to be a clairvoyant. How to catch a man who was.

The others could have helped but Penn had blocked that. With a dozen other clairvoyants Don could have covered the field and trapped Klieger by sheer weight of numbers. No one man, no matter how gifted, could have beaten such odds.

Now he was on his own.

It had begun to rain and the window glittered with reflected light, so that his eyes constantly changed focus from the window to the city beyond, then back to the window. Then he stopped trying to focus and just stood there, eyes wide, thoughts travelling unfamiliar paths.

How?

How did he know when and where to catch a wanted man? What was it that made him just that little different from other men? All his life Don had had that edge. He could guess — if it was guessing — and those guesses had been right. So, was it guessing? Or did he know?

His record had backed his application to the C.I.A. That same record of unbroken success had paved his way into the Special Detachment. He was a man-hunter who always found his man. And he didn't know how he did it.

As Malchin didn't know how the 'residents' at Cartwright House used their talents.

29

Even whittled down the list was too long. Earlman gestured towards the map, smoke drifting from the cigarette dangling from his lips, pointing to the varicoloured pins.

'I can't get it closer than this, Don. From here on it's pure guesswork.'

'Not quite.' Don scanned the list. 'I learned something about Klieger back at Cartwright House. He is an artistic type. My guess is that he's been visiting the museums and art galleries all along.'

'Then we've got him!' Earlman was jubilant. 'All we need do is cover these places and he'll walk right into our hands.'

Don raised his eyebrows and Max suddenly sobered.

'No. Every cop in the city has his photograph and description. All routes from the metropolis are covered. All field units are on the hunt. If it was as easy as that, we'd have had him by now.' He gestured towards the map. 'Then why all this?'

'Concentration of effort.' Don sat on the edge of a bed. 'The cops can't spot him until they see him, and he makes certain they don't. Mostly he's just one man in a crowd and that's the best disguise there is. Never forget, Max, he can 'see' our traps and so avoid them.'

'Then it's hopeless.' Savagely Earlman stamped on his cigarette. 'No matter what we do, where we go, he won't be there. Have I wasted my time, Don?'

'No.'

'But — '

'It's between him and me now,' said Don. 'Up until now I've tackled this like a slightly abnormal operation. I've depended on outside help and even tried to get special assistance but that wasn't the way to do it. Now I've got to use his weakness against him.' He looked down at the list in his hand.

'All right, both of you get out, I want to be alone.'

Bronson didn't move.

'You heard the man!' Earlman jerked open the door. 'Out!'

Slowly Bronson rose to his feet. His eyes shone as he stared at Don.

'I'm not going anywhere,' said Gregson

tiredly. 'You can wait outside if you want.'

Alone he untied his shoes, loosened his tie and slipped off his jacket. Killing the lights he lay back on the bed, eyes towards the window with its glitter of reflected light. Deliberately he relaxed.

For him it was a normal procedure, this quiet relaxation while his mind digested the thousand odd items of assembled fact to come up with a guess that wasn't a guess because it was always right. But now he had to do more than that. Now he had to pit himself against a man who could 'see' the future and he had to outguess that other man.

His breathing grew even, regular and deeper as he entered the first stage of self-hypnosis. Outside sounds wouldn't bother him now, there would be no distractions, he could concentrate fully on the problem he had to solve.

Find Klieger.

Find where he would be and when.

Find him as he had found a thousand others with no doubt, no uncertainty, just the conviction that at a certain place at a certain time he would spot his quarry.

Forget the sense that he was beaten before he could start. Forget that he was up against an abnormal talent. Forget the picture of the piece of fabric and the nodes of events. Forget everything but one man and where and when he would be.

★ ★ ★

'The Lustrum Galleries.' Earlman nodded then grunted as the cab braked to avoid a jaywalker. 'They are having a private showing this evening, invitation only. The exhibition doesn't open until tomorrow.' He looked at Don, face even more haggard in the dim light. 'Are you certain he will be there?'

'Yes.'

'But — ' Earlman shrugged and broke off, killing the obvious question. 'A display of Chinese art,' he read from a crumpled catalogue. 'Ceramics from the Ming, Han and Manchu Dynasties. It figures. The Ming vase?'

Don nodded, then closed his eyes, resting his head on the back of the seat. He felt drained, worn out yet filled with a glowing exultation. He knew! How or why he couldn't guess but he knew! Klieger would be at the galleries. He would stake his life on it.

Their badges got them in, past a very punctilious uniformed attendant, past a fussing curator, into a long hall shining with glass cases on which in reverent array stood the exhibits.

'Tomorrow,' said the curator, 'these will be within the cases but tonight, because of the selected visitors, we feel it safe to have them as they are.'

'Why?' Earlman was blunt. 'What's the point?'

'You are not a connoisseur,' said the curator. 'That is obvious. If you were, you would know that there is more to ceramics than just the visual aspect. There is a feel, a tactile sense that is as much a part of the pottery as the colors. Our visitors, most of them collectors, appreciate that. And, too, the true beauty of these pieces cannot be wholly appreciated when they are seen from only one angle as they will be when sealed in the cases.'

He looked suddenly anxious.

'You haven't mentioned your business. I trust that nothing will — '

'There will be no trouble.' Don glanced around the gallery, forehead creased in a frown. 'Just operate as if we weren't here.' He smiled at the anxious expression. 'One thing I can promise you, your exhibits are in no danger.'

Satisfied, the curator bustled off about his business. Don glanced to either side then led the way towards the far end of the gallery.

'We'll wait here. The cases will screen us and we can watch the whole gallery. When Klieger comes you will go to the stairs, Max, and cut off his escape.'

Earlman grunted then paused, a cigarette halfway to his lips.

'How come, Don? How come Klieger is going to walk right into this set-up when we know that he must know we're waiting for him?'

'He wants to see the exhibits.'

'But — ?'

'This is his only chance to actually touch and examine them. To him that's important, don't ask me why.' Don's voice was sharp. 'He'll be here, I know it.'

It sounded logical. It sounded as if it could be true but Don knew that wasn't the reason Klieger would come. He would want to see the ceramics, that was true, but would he want to handle them so much that nothing else mattered? And, if so, why? Why tonight?

Waiting between the cases, eyes on the long vista of the gallery with its shining glass and neat exhibits Don fought the question that had puzzled him all along. In a way it was a seeming paradox, but he knew that it only seemed that way to him. As the visitors began to arrive and the air vibrated to their murmured comments as they studied the exhibits the question nagged at his peace of mind.

Klieger must know he would be walking into a trap.

Yet he would come, Don was certain of it.

So, if Don wasn't mistaken and he was certain he was not, Klieger must consider the visit to be worth certain capture.

Capture or —

Bronson moved, an automatic gesture,

36

one hand sliding beneath his coat, and Don snarled at him with savage impatience.

'There'll be none of that! Do you understand? You won't be needed!'

Inwardly he cursed Penn's cold, inhuman logic. In war it is good sense to destroy material you can't use to prevent it falling into enemy hands, but this wasn't war and Penn wasn't dealing with machines or supplies.

Klieger must know the risk he ran of being shot to death.

Don started as Earlman gripped his arm. Max jerked his head, eyes bright in the haggard face as he stared down the gallery.

'There, Don,' he breathed. 'Down by that big case. See him?'

Klieger!

He was — ordinary. Engrossed with the hunt Don had mentally fitted the quarry with supernatural peculiarities but now, watching him as he stood, entranced by pottery fired before the dawn of Western civilization, he seemed nothing but what he was. An ordinary man with more than an ordinary interest in things considered beautiful by a minority.

And yet he had knowledge, which made him the most dangerous man to the security of the West.

'Got him!' Earlman's whisper was triumphant. 'You did it again, Don! You called it right on the nose!'

'Get into position.' Gregson didn't take his eyes from the slight figure he had hunted so long. 'Stand by in case he makes a break for it. You know what to do.'

'I know.' Earlman hesitated. 'Bronson?'

'I'll take care of him.'

Don waited as Earlman slipped away, gliding past the cases to lean casually at the top of the far stairs. He sensed the other's relief and understood it. They had worked together for eight years and his failure would, in part, have been shared by Earlman.

But he had not failed.

Savouring the sweet taste of success he walked forward half-conscious of Bronson at his heels. Klieger did not turn. He stood, caressing a shallow, wide-mouthed bowl in his hands, eyes intent on the still-bright colours.

'Klieger!'

Slowly he set down the vase.

'Don't run. Don't fight. Don't do anything stupid.' Don's voice was a grim whisper. 'You can't get away.'

'I know.'

'Just in case you're wondering I'm from the C.I.A.'

'I know.'

'This is the end of the line, Klieger.'

'I know.'

The calm, emotionless tones irritated Gregson. The man should have complained, argued, anything but the flat baldness of the repeated statement. Savagely he gripped a shoulder and spun Klieger round to face him.

'Do you know everything?'

Klieger didn't answer. Heavy lids dropped over the eyes and Don remembered how Levkin had described them. 'Remarkable' the owner had said, but the word was misleading. They were haunted. There was no other description, no other word. Haunted.

'What are you going to do with me?'

Klieger opened his eyes and stared up into the grim face of the hunter. Don shrugged.

'Why ask? You're the man who is supposed to know everything.'

'I am a clairvoyant,' said Klieger calmly. 'I can see into the future, but so can you. Do you know everything?'

'I — ' Don swallowed. 'What did you say?'

'How else would you have known that I would be here? And I mean know, not guess. You were certain that you would find me, as certain as I am that — '

'Go on.'

'You have the talent. By knowing that I would be here at this time you 'saw' into the future. Not far, perhaps, but too clearly, but you 'saw'. What other proof do you need?'

'But I simply had a conviction that — Is that how clairvoyancy works?'

'For you, obviously yes. For others perhaps not exactly the same. But when you are convinced beyond any shadow of doubt that at a certain time a thing will happen, or that a thing will happen even if the exact time is not too precise, then you have the gift which General Penn values most highly.' Klieger gave a bitter smile. 'Much good may it do you.'

Don shook his head, conscious of receiving knowledge too fast and too soon. At his elbow Bronson shifted his weight a little, poising on the balls of his feet. Around them was a clear space as the other visitors moved down the line of cases. The three of them stood in an island of isolation.

'I am not coming back with you,' announced Klieger. 'I have had enough of Cartwright House.'

'You have no choice.'

Klieger smiled. 'You forget,' he pointed out gently, 'it isn't a question of choice. It is a simple question of knowledge. I shall never see the general again.'

Bronson made an incoherent sound deep in his throat.

He was fast, incredibly fast, but Don was even faster. Warned by some unknown sense he spun as the gun flashed into view, snatching at the wrist as it swung level, twisting and forcing the black muzzle from its target with viciously applied leverage. Muscles knotted then the bone snapped with the dry sound of a breaking stick. Bronson opened his mouth as the gun fell from nerveless fingers then Don slashed the hard edge of his palm across the nerves in the neck and the mute collapsed.

Quickly Don scooped up the gun and heaved Bronson to his feet, supporting the unconscious man as he fought mounting tides of hate. Hate for Bronson who lived only to take revenge on the world for his disability. Hatred for Penn who could find a use for the psychopathic mute and others like him. Licensed murderers in the sacred name of expediency; safe because they could never talk.

Earlman had seen what the others in the gallery had not. Running forward he met the blaze of Gregson's eyes.

'Get rid of this thing, fast!'

'So he had to try it.' Earlman relieved Don of the dead weight. 'Penn is going to love you for this.'

Don sucked air, fighting to rid himself of hate. 'Take him back to the hotel. I'll worry about Penn when I have to.'

'And Klieger?'

'I'll take care of him.'

Don had almost forgotten Klieger in the savage fury of the past few minutes. He found him standing by one of the exhibits, staring at a relic of the past as if he were trying to drink its beauty and impress its image on his brain. Gently he picked up the piece, a man entranced by the artistic perfection of ancient craftsmen and, looking at him, Don felt his stomach tighten with a sudden, sick understanding.

★   ★   ★

Penn didn't trust women. The receptionist was a man as were all his personnel. He took one look at Don then lunged for a buzzer.

'Why bother?' Don headed past him towards the inner office. 'Just tell the general that I'm on my way in.'

'But — ?'

'How did I get this far without being stopped?' Don shrugged. 'You figure it out.'

Penn wasn't alone. Earlman, more haggard than ever, sat smoking unhappily and Don guessed that he had been receiving the full weight of the general's anger. He grinned as the door slammed shut behind him.

'Hi, Max, you look as if you've been having a bad time.'

'Don!' Earlman lunged to his feet. 'Where have you been? It's more than a week now. Where's Klieger?'

'Klieger.' Don smiled. 'At this moment he is somewhere in Soviet territory being interrogated by every lie-detection device known to man.'

For a moment there was a deathly silence then Penn leaned forward.

'All right, Gregson, you've had your joke. Now produce Klieger or take the consequences.'

'It's no joke.' Don stared grimly into the general's eyes. 'That's what I've been doing this past week. Talking to Klieger, fixing his passage, dodging your hunters.'

'Traitor!'

Don didn't answer.

'You dirty, stinking traitor!' Suddenly Penn became icy calm and his calmness was more terrible than his rage. 'This is a

Democracy, Gregson, but we know how to protect ourselves. You should have gone with Klieger to the safety of your friends.'

'Friends! You think I did it for them?' Don looked down at his hands, they were shaking. Deliberately he sat down, lit a cigarette, waited for his anger to pass.

'You demand loyalty,' he said. 'Blind, unswerving, unthinking loyalty. You think that those who are not with you must be for the enemy but you are wrong. There is a greater loyalty than to an individual, a nation or a group of nations. There is a loyalty to the human race. One day, please God, both sides may realize that.'

'Don!'

Earlman leaned forward. Gregson gestured him back to his chair,

'Just listen, Max, you too, General. Listen and try to understand.'

He paused, dragging at the cigarette, his broad-planed face revealing some of his fatigue.

'The answer,' he said, 'lay in the Ming vase.'

'The one Klieger stole from the antique

45

shop?' Earlman nodded. 'What about it, Don? Why was it so important?'

He was, Don knew, acting as a barrier between him and the wrath of the general and he was suddenly glad that he was there. Penn, alone, might never have found the patience to listen.

'Klieger can see into the future,' continued Don. 'Never forget that. He was the star 'resident' at Cartwright House and stayed there for ten years. Then, for no apparent reason, he decided to take off. He did. He stole money — he had to live, and he stole a vase, to him a thing of wondrous beauty. The answer lies in why he did it.'

'A thief!' Penn snorted. 'He was a thief. That's the answer.'

'No,' said Don quietly. 'The reason is that time was running out — and he knew it!'

They stared at him. They didn't understand, not even Earlman, certainly not Penn and yet, to Don, it was all clear. So ghastly clear.

'What a man does is determined by his character,' said Don. 'Given a certain

stimulus he will react in a certain way
— and this is predictable. Think of
Klieger and what he was. Meek, mild,
inoffensive, willing to do as he was told
without question. He did it for ten years
while his talent was being trained so that
he could 'see' further and clearer into the
future. Then one day he 'sees' something
that drives him desperate.

'Desperate enough to break the habits
of a lifetime. He persuaded the others to
help him escape. They thought that he
was doing it to help them, perhaps they
wanted to prove something, that isn't
important now. Klieger is. He walked out.
He stole. He tried to fill every waking
hour with what he considered to be the
ultimate of beauty. A different man would
have gambled, drank, chased women.
Klieger loves old and precious things. He
stole a Ming vase.'

'Why?' Despite himself Penn was interested.

'Because he saw the ultimate war!'

Don leaned forward, his cigarette
forgotten, his eyes burning with the
necessity of making them see what he

knew was the truth.

'He saw the end of everything. He saw his own death and he wanted, poor devil, to live a little before he died.'

It made sense. Even to Penn it made sense. He had seen the secret records, the breakdown of a man's character, the psychological dissection and extrapolations. Security was very thorough.

'I — ' Penn swallowed. 'I can't believe it.'

'It's the truth.' Don remembered his cigarette. 'He told me — we had plenty of time for talking. How else do you think we managed to catch him? He could have remained free forever had he tried. But he was tired, afraid, terrified. He wanted to see the exhibition and he expected to die by Bronson's bullet.'

'Now wait a minute!' Earlman frowned, a crease folding his forehead. 'No man in his right mind would willingly go to his death. It doesn't make sense.'

'No?' Don was grim. 'Think about it.'

'A bullet is quick and clean,' mused Earlman. 'But he didn't die! Bronson was stopped!'

'That is why I turned 'traitor'.' Don crushed out his cigarette. 'By stopping Bronson I proved that the future is a variable, that even an expert clairvoyant like Klieger can only see the probable future, not the inevitable one. It gave us hope. Both of us.'

He rose, looking down at Penn slumped behind his desk, trying not to let the hate he saw in the general's eyes disturb him. He had no need to worry.

'I had no choice. The pattern must be broken if we are to avoid the future Klieger saw. So I gave him to the Reds — he was willing to do his part. They will learn the truth.'

'They will copy us!' Penn reared to his feet. 'They will form their own project and we will lose our greatest advantage. Gregson, do you know what you have done?'

'I've opened a window to the future — for them as well as for us. Now there will be no ultimate war.'

'Smart!' Penn didn't trouble to hide his sneer. 'You're so smart! You've taken it on yourself to do this without authority. I'll see you dead for this!'

'No, General.' Don shook his head. 'You won't see me dead.'

'That's what you think. I'll have you shot!'

Don smiled, warm in the comforting knowledge of his new awareness.

'No,' he said. 'You won't have me shot.'

TROJAN HORSE

Marlo French woke, shivering, immediately conscious of the freezing chill. Rising he touched the radiator. Cold. In the bathroom icy water gushed from faucets which should have delivered hot. Snarling he padded into the living room, hit the switches of radio, percolator and fire. Music rose as he yelled at the phone. 'Get me the manager!'

He didn't recognise the face that looked at him from the screen. 'Can I be of service, sir?'

'The radiator's cold,' said Marlo. 'The water. The damn place is like an iceberg. Am I being given special treatment?'

'No, sir, but — '

'You're not the manager. Where's Hardy?'

'I am the assistant manager, sir.'

'Not good enough. Get Hardy.'

The fire was glowing red by the time he arrived. He looked pale, distraught. His left arm was cradled in a black sling. 'My apologies, sir. I am terribly sorry for the inconvenience but the trouble will be rectified as soon as possible.'

Marlo scowled. 'It shouldn't have happened. Am I supposed to catch pneumonia or something?'

Hardy looked embarrassed. 'The truth is, Mr. French,' he said with a burst of candour, 'we had a little trouble last night. An attempted takeover. It failed, of course, but they managed to get into the boiler room and some pipes got damaged. I had to shut off the steam in order to effect repairs but everything is now under control.' He hesitated. 'Your tolerance would be highly appreciated, Mr. French.'

'The hell with that,' snapped Marlo. 'With the rent I pay why should I be tolerant? Credit me a day and get the heat on fast!'

He killed the phone and stood warming himself before the fire. Some takeover! They hadn't even cut the power or perhaps they had and Hardy had managed to get it reconnected. Most probably it had been a gang of zanies on a raid or even a breakdown and the manager was making excuses. He remembered the sling. Well, maybe not, but even if the attempt had been genuine it didn't solve the problem of his shower.

He compromised, turning up the radio before going into the bathroom, washing face and neck and depilating his cheeks. The cream ran out before he'd covered all the stubble and he finished the job with a razor managing to nick a cheek. Scowling he examined the wound. It was slight but messy and made his lean, saturnine features even more sinister. Irritably he dabbed the cut with styptic and went to dress. He was checking his gun when the phone rang.

Holstering the weapon he looked at the information display below the blank screen. Ed Whalen, High Boss of Chicago Chemicals, a top-graded character with a high reliability index and strong protective affiliations. Marlo flipped the switch.

'French?' Whalen was in his late middle-age with deep-set eyes and a strong, heavily jowled face. 'Marlo French?'

'That's right.'

'I want to see you.'

'You're looking.'

'I mean personally. This is business, Are you interested in making money or not?'

Marlo glanced at the information panel below the screen of the phone. The computer memory system had dug a little deeper and had analysed the emotional index of the caller. Whalen was at a high pitch of nervous tension, seething with frustrated anger, almost hysterical and on the very edge of panic-reaction. 'I'm interested,' he said. 'But I can't afford to throw away time. Can't you tell me what it is over the phone?'

'No,' snapped Whalen. 'I'm at the plant. Be there within the hour and you won't regret it.'

★ ★ ★

He sat in an office buried three hundred feet below the surface. The elevator was equipped with both spy and exterminating devices; the passage leading from it rigged with electronic bloodhounds. Marlo had to deposit his gun, knife and rings before he could pass into the office. Whalen rose as he entered. 'You want something? A drink?'

Marlo shook his head and glanced around the office as Whalen crossed to where bottles stood on a tray. The place reeked of luxury. The carpet was ankle deep, the ceiling a miniature replica of that in the Sistine Chapel, the furniture of real, hand-worked wood. Living murals gave the impression of actual scenes. Skiers on a mountain slope, camels on a desert, naked women swimming in the sea. One of them, a blonde, winked at him.

'All right,' said Marlo as Whalen walked towards him. 'Why me?'

'I don't get you.'

'Let's not play games,' said Marlo tiredly. 'Chicago Chemicals is big enough to have all kinds on its payroll. Trouble-shooters, assassins, the lot. If you had to you could raise a private army so — why me?'

Whalen sipped at his drink. 'You've a good reputation. You're shrewd, smart, reliable. A man who knows how to be discreet and one with no interest in inter-firm politics. And — '

'I'm expendable,' interrupted Marlo. 'All right, I've got the picture. You want something done and you want it kept private. What's the problem?'

Whalen finished his drink and helped himself to another. 'It's a matter of recovery. Something was taken from our research laboratory and I want it back.'

Marlo waited.

'Wayne, my head chemist, has been working on a new compound. The initial test-batch was a hundred and fifty pills, lime-green in colour and two millimetres in diameter. One hundred and twenty-three of them were left after preliminary tests. Someone took them. I want them back.'

'And fast,' guessed Marlo, 'before who has them can get them analysed. Am I warm?'

'Almost red hot,' admitted Whalen. 'Wayne hadn't bothered to introduce any blocking elements and unrecognisable non-essentials so as to safeguard the product. Any chemist who knows his stuff could break down the compound and discover the formula.'

'Now tell me the rest of it,' urged Marlo. 'Who it is who took the stuff and why you can't just reach out and take it back. The whole thing.' He frowned as Whalen hesitated. 'Look,' he said coldly. 'If you expect me to believe that a stranger walked into your laboratory, helped himself to something you consider valuable and simply walked out again you must think I'm crazy. Whoever it was took the stuff couldn't have been a stranger. It must be someone belonging to the firm and with right of entry because you'd have that place guarded at all times. So you must know who it is. And yet you send for me. Why?'

'I told you.'

'That's right,' said Marlo sourly. 'I'm expendable.'

'Not that,' corrected Whalen. 'Discreet.' He looked at the glass then impatiently put it down on his desk. 'The person who took those pills is my daughter.'

Marlo nodded. 'That figures.'

'I discovered the loss and immediately

checked the surveillance-system,' continued Whalen. 'There were images and other means of identification. Naomi worked here and had the right of entry. For her it would have been easy to take the stuff.'

'And easy for you to take back?'

'No!' Whelan's seething anger bubbled close to the surface and drove him to pace the floor. 'As yet it's been impossible! I haven't seen her,' he explained. 'She refuses to communicate. There seems to be no way I can get hold of her short of an outright war. Damn it, French! You've got to help me!'

'I'll help you,' promised Marlo. 'But it's going to cost you a lot of money.' He paused, thinking. 'Let me get this straight. Naomi has the stuff. She won't talk to you and is somewhere where you can't get at her. Right?'

'She's in the Staysafe Apartments,' said Whalen. 'I know that for certain.'

Marlo pursed his lips. 'I take it that she has protective affiliations so if you tried an outright raid things would get out of hand. But what if they did?' He snapped his fingers. 'Got it! That stuff she took — you want it kept secret. You daren't chance her spreading the information and if you make an attack that's just what she'll do. So you want me to get it back all nice and quietly. And if I have to kill her to get it?'

'You kill her,' said Whalen.

'Your own daughter?'

'Sure. Why not?'

'No reason,' admitted Marlo. 'I just wanted to be sure.'

* * *

The bed was a sea, a warm, scented, beautiful ocean, yielding, protecting, enfolding her in a miniature universe as snug and as comfortable as a womb. Naomi Whalen stirred, stretching, arching her back, eyes closed as she ran her hands over the febrile skin of her naked body. Desire was a living flame. Eyes still closed she reached out, felt the warm firmness of male contours, dug her nails deep into the surrogate muscles of the back.

'Darling!' The voice was soft, low, a

husky whisper of passion. 'I love you, my darling! I need you. I long to possess your body.'

Her hands moved, nails digging a familiar pattern, preset controls yielding beneath their impact. The mannikin stirred, fluids coursing to produce an artificial perspiration, a growing tumescence. The limbs arranged themselves into a position of dominance, the respiration increased, synthetic passion faithfully duplicated.

'Talk to me!' she demanded. 'Talk to me!'

Triggered by the sonic command the mannikin's voice deepened, quickened, whispering a succession of image-producing concepts, obscenities, vulgar colloquialisms all calculated to induce maximum erotic response. The woman groaned in pleasure. As a lover the mannikin was unequalled because it was an extension of herself, programmed to do and say the things she most desired. And it was untiring.

Satiated she commanded the mannikin to quiescence and sat upright in the bed. The apartment was warm, comfortable, an extension of the womb-bed. She rose, prowled the rooms, nerves jumping as they always did when she looked for signs of danger. The phone rang as she headed towards the bathroom; the display told her that her father was calling again. She smiled as she read the emotional data. A little more and he would burst a blood-vessel or run wild and get himself shot. To hell with him.

She took her time over the shower, using plenty of deodorants and perfumes, brushing the long mane of hair until it shone like polished gold. Dressed in a lounging suit that made the most of her legs and figure she fixed breakfast, using food from sealed cans. Curiosity made her switch on the window, the repeater screen fed from a scanner on the roof. The weather was lousy, cold rain driving from the lake and giving promise of a hard winter.

She dropped her coffee cup as the door-chime sounded.

'Miss Whalen.' The corridor-guard was punctiliously polite. His face on the door-screen was lined and solemn. 'The usual check, Miss Whalen. Is everything all right?'

'Yes.'

'I can't see you, Miss Whalen. Will you please activate your screen.' His eyes blinked as she did so. 'Thank you.'

'Nurd,' she said.

'Thank you, Miss Whalen.' The check was complete. The code word had told him that she was quite safe, that no one was crouched out of sight threatening her with a weapon. 'Will you be needing the cleaners today?'

'No.'

He touched the stiff visor of his helmet and turned away. At midday he or another would repeat the check. It would be done again in late afternoon, again at evening. At night the building was sealed like a vault with guards personally accompanying residents to their rooms. The Staysafe Apartments lived up to their reputation.

The phone rang, the display signalling that the caller was a Julia Weston of the Lonely Lesbians, emotional index neutral. Naomi let it ring. During the next two hours she had calls from the Self-Satisfiers Society, the Church of the Hidden Truth, an agency specialising in weapon-implants, a mutual protection group and someone who had a perverted need to scream abuse at anyone he could get to listen. Finally she rang the manager.

'Yes, Miss Whalen?'

'I'm being assaulted,' she said coldly. 'Bothered by a lot of nurds ringing me up. What's happened to your filter?'

'Nothing, Miss Whalen. I'm sorry if you've been inconvenienced but you did ask that all calls be routed right through. Would you like to change that instruction?'

'No,' she said. 'Forget it.'

Turning she saw the mannikin. It looked back at her, electronic magic giving the eyes a semblance of life so that, oddly, she felt a momentary embarrassment.

'Go to sleep,' she ordered.

Obediently the eyelids fluttered, the lashes coming to rest on the cheeks. Almost imperceptibly the chest rose and fell, so that, to anyone unknowing, the mannikin looked exactly like a young and handsome man in a light and natural sleep.

When not on active duty the thing made an excellent watchdog.

Connors Lacey, Professor of Deportment, examined his class as they arrived for the morning session. Young men all eager to get up and on. With satisfaction he noted they all kept plenty of distance between each other. Waiting until they had squatted on the padded floor he advanced the rostrum, mounted, looked down at his pupils.

'Good morning,' he said politely. 'I trust you have all had a pleasant night's sleep?'

All but one chorused their agreement. Connors glanced at him, checked his status on the rostrum display. Phillip Wayne, chief of the research department of Chicago Chemicals. A young man to hold such a position and obviously with something on his mind.

'Wayne!' snapped Connors. 'I asked you a question.'

'Go to hell!'

Connors moved. A gun appeared in his hand, the hammer falling with a loud click. Had the weapon been loaded Wayne would now be dead.

'Once again I emphasise the primary lesson of survival,' said Connors. He was shaking a little; rudeness always threw him into a killing rage. 'Politeness is cheap and yet more lives have been saved by the use of a little courtesy than by all the protack ever taught. A man who avoids a fight has an immediate advantage over a man who has to win one. In your position, dealing as you do with people of aggressive natures, you will find that the use of politeness is a better weapon than all your guns, knives, gas and combat skills. A better defence than your padded caps and metal-lined clothing. In the field of social activity, as in the field of medicine, prevention is better than cure.'

He paused, became aware that he still held the pistol and threw it on the lectern. 'To sum up,' he said, emphasising every word, 'The real secret of success lies in the exercise of self-control.'

One of the class had an objection. 'Surely that can't be right. If a man's coming at you with a knife, what's the good of being polite?'

'None,' admitted Connors patiently.

How the hell did some of these nurds ever get their jobs? 'If someone is coming at you, you don't think — you react. But I was talking about prevention. What made the man blow his top in the first place? Maybe you did. Self-control could have prevented the situation. Think,' he insisted. 'Think before you act.'

'The thalmic pause,' said one of the class brightly. He sat towards the rear and carried MACE fed to a lapel-spray, the weapon triggered by toe-pressure. 'Professor Hay was telling us about it in psychology.'

'He wasn't talking about the same thing,' said Connors patiently. 'Now listen. I call you a nurd — what do you do?'

'If you meant it I'd smash your face in,' said one.

'Shove a blade in your guts,' said another.

A third was even more terse. 'Kick,' he said.

Connors speared the first speaker with his finger. 'You,' he said. 'How would you know if I meant it or not?'

The pupil blinked.

'You would have exercised self-control,' said Connors triumphantly. 'You would have paused to think. Did I mean what I said? Was it an insult and did it call for action? If so would you have the advantage? An assessment of the probabilities,' he summed up. 'A moment of time in which to study the situation. Learn to do that and you have world by the tail.'

The pupil who carried MACE frowned. 'Now wait a minute. You're talking about the censor. Professor Hay told us all about it. How it used to be a barrier between thought and action. How people used to resist their emotional drives, or if they didn't, used to be classified as dangerously insane. Are you saying that we should redevelop it?'

'Certainly not!' Connors was disgusted at the suggestion. 'The censor was the worst thing which could have happened to the human race. What I am talking about isn't a built-in barrier between desire and action but a voluntary process of self-discipline by which we gain a choice of action. The difference is important. In the days when the race was cursed with an operative censor a man had no real freedom of choice when it came to action. He would still feel desire, hate, hunger, all the normal emotions on the subconscious level but, before they could reach the conscious level the censor had done his work. Instead of a healthy reaction the man would be frustrated by that diabolical barrier. The result, of course, was a slave-mentality and an insane culture.

'Now we no longer have the censor. A man reacts to his emotional stimulus without any hampering restrictions. But that does not mean we must do without self-control. I call you an insulting name. Without training you will react in a predictable manner and seek to kill or injure me because I have aroused a hate-response. Now, if you can still feel that response but do not need to immediately react the advantages are obvious.' He pointed to a member of the class. 'Name one.'

'You could wait until he isn't looking then give it to him,' said the man.

'Right.' The finger moved. 'You! Give me another.'

'You could wait until the next time you met and then give it to him.'

'You're extending, not inventing,' said Connors. He pointed to Wayne. 'You!'

'You'd become an enigma,' said the chemist slowly. 'Unpredictable and therefore dangerous and all the more respected.'

Connors nodded. 'Very good. At least you have imagination.' He clapped his hands. 'That's enough theory for today. Let's get on with some practice. Don't forget that the art of protack is to couple both attack and defence. Now, take partners and begin. Left side, thumb to the eye and knee to the groin. Right side, knock aside thumb, twist to avoid knee, respond with kick to ankle and chop to side of neck. Left side . . . '

They were a good class. A quarter of them would probably be dead before they rose from junior executive status but the rest should make it. Some of them might even reach old age.

★ ★ ★

71

The place smelt of perfume, of smoke and tweed and things masculine together with a subtle blend of rinse and powder and the skin-scents of women. Fragile chairs stood on a carpet of neutral grey. Soft fabrics lined the walls. A kaleidobulb threw a wash of ever-changing coloured light over the ceiling and through the air. Against the pastel softness Marlo felt big and hard and grittily out of place.

'My dear sir!' Quentin Quail, middle-aged, bouncing, a little too full in the rear and a little too narrow in the chest, hair impossibly neat in mathematical disarray, hands white and plump and gesturing. 'Do be seated! Do relax! Do have confidence! I know exactly what you need!'

'You do?' Marlo took a chair.

'But, of course! A man like yourself, someone of sensitivity and imagination, a man who has depths it would take a normal partner a lifetime to plumb. Gentle and strong, generous and firm, ruthless and yet with an infinite capacity for understanding. Yes, my dear sir, I know exactly what you need.'

Marlo smiled. 'Tell me.'

'A brunette, Mr. French,' gushed Quail. 'But why should we restrict ourselves? A composite,' he decided. 'A model with variable-toned hair so that you may enjoy the pleasure of an infinite range of colour from silver to jet. Just think of it! Ash blonde, honey, stimulating russet, warm auburn, tantalising brown and rippling coils of lustrous black.' Quail sighed, hands shaping the air. 'It costs a trifle more, but think of the tremendous variety. And, after all, what is money?'

'Something to spend,' said Marlo. 'But — '

'A man of the world,' interrupted Quail, lost in a salesman's dream. 'I sensed it as soon as you stepped through the door. My technicians, I told myself, will have to work hard to satisfy this gentleman. They will need all their skill and cunning to satisfy his educated tastes. But, my dear sir, they willingly accept the challenge. No effort is too great for someone as appreciative as yourself. Some wine?'

He danced from the room before Mario could answer, returned with a bottle and two glasses poised precariously on a tray. 'Champagne,' he said. 'Real wine made from genuine grapes and reserved, need I say, for those who are able to appreciate a true vintage.' He poured, sipped, looked thoughtfully over the rim of his glass.

'Now that we have settled the question of the hair I think it would be best to go the whole way and build you a special construction. The advantages are so great I do not for one moment even consider the possibility of your refusal. Sophistication,' said Quail putting down his glass, so as to give free rein to his hands. 'When we are not confined by limitations of price true artistry comes into its own. The height can be variable up to six inches. The mammary development to eight and the hips the same. This will give you a choice from near-nymphet to junoesque and permit an interesting arrangement of combinations. More wine, Mr. French?'

'Why not?' said Marlo.

'And now we come to skin tones.' Quail looked at the ceiling and kissed the tips of his fingers. 'A world of women rolled into

74

one. Like the hair the colour of the skin can range from white to black; shades controllable from albino to African negroid with a selector mechanism to govern racial characteristics. And, naturally, there will be all the usual refinements plus a few rather unusual combinations I am certain you will find engrossing.' Quail managed to convey the impression of winking without actually closing an eye. 'You may trust me, Mr. French. I shall build you the finest femmikin ever seen in this or any other age.'

'Thank you,' said Marlo patiently. 'But I don't want a femmikin. I've been trying to tell you that.'

Quail was immediately understanding. 'Not to worry, my dear sir. The same advantages I have enumerated can, naturally, be incorporated into a mannikin. To ensure complete satisfaction I would strongly advise that you place yourself unreservedly into the hands of my psycho-technicians so that your deepest yearnings can be discovered and appropriate responses built into the model. We can start work on the transfer of fifty per cent of the estimated price.'

'I'm sure you can,' said Marlo, 'but I don't want a mannikin, either.'

Quail gurgled. 'Then what do you want?'

Marlo told him.

As a plan it was simple but Marlo liked the simple plans — there was less to go wrong. And there had been a precedent, a good one. Discovering that Naomi owned a mannikin had been a routine checking of credit transfer. Guessing who had made it was a matter of elimination; Quail was the best in the business and she would have had nothing but the best. Getting him to agree to making the match was the hard part.

Hard but not impossible. Every man had his price and Quail was no exception. It was a high price but Whalen was paying. All Marlo was risking was his neck.

Quail was positively eager now that he'd been bought and paid for. He led Marlo into a room scented with antiseptics and watched him strip.

'A good body,' he mused. 'But we'll have to disguise that scar tissue. A general skin-tone will take care of that scar with any other blemishes.' He prodded Marlo as if he'd been a horse, gripping the stomach, nodding as he felt the slabs of hard muscle. 'A little surplus fat,' he murmured, 'but we've time to sweat that off. Let's check your measurements.'

Quail frowned over a sheaf of photographs.

'You're about the right height,' he said. 'The extra inch won't matter. Neither will the slight difference in musculature. We'll have to do something about the face and hair and you'll have quite a bit to learn from the tapes.' He picked up a hypodermic syringe. 'Turn around and keep still.'

Marlo felt a template touch his skin then grunted as the needle plunged repeatedly into his back. 'What's that for?'

'The control studs,' explained Quail. 'The real ones are plastic set beneath the skin but these are nodules of testosterone which will become assimilated in time.' He chuckled like a satyr. 'You should feel quite an improvement in certain abilities soon.' The needle dug in again, this time higher towards the nape of the skull. 'And this is the emergency stop button. Press it and the mannikin will freeze. Most customers insist on it. It gives them a feeling of confidence.'

'It's given me a sore back,' said Marlo. 'What next?'

A dentist did things to his mouth, an optician worked on his eyes, a hairdresser his hair. Two women concentrated on his face, moulding surrogate flesh, injecting absorbants that could be shaped, spraying and touching until Quail nodded his satisfaction.

There were tapes, recordings of Naomi's subconscious desires that had been incorporated into the response-mechanism of the mannikin. Marlo memorised them, then practised adjusting his voice until the tones made a vibration pattern which matched a wavering line on a screen.

'Good,' said Quail finally. 'Mr. French, you are almost an identical facsimile of Miss Naomi Whalen's mannikin. Two things you must bear in mind. The first is not to get carried away. Do nothing that is not programmed on the tapes. You are, after all, supposed to be a machine. The other is not to stay too long. Fake a breakdown. She will call me and I'll make the reverse switch.' He glanced at his watch. 'Soon we shall be ready to move. Are you quite comfortable, Mr. French?'

Marlo nodded. His face and neck were stiff from applied cosmetics, his back itched from the injections and his head ached from forced tuition but, aside from that, he felt fine. 'Have you made arrangements for the exchange?'

'I have.' Quail pursed his lips. 'Miss Whalen was most difficult to contact and even more difficult to persuade. However she accepted the fact that a small but vital component in her mannikin needs to be immediately replaced. Reluctantly she agreed to release her friend for a short while. Soon we shall be taking it — you — back to her.'

And then would come the hard part.

* * *

Marlo heard the sound of the doorchime, the exchange of words, the slight rumble as the handlers rolled in his crate. The lid lifted and fingernails dug into his back. Obediently be stepped forward. The handlers backed away together with Quail and the guards. The door closed. Feet padded softly over the carpet and he caught the scent of perfume.

'Darling,' said Naomi. 'Open your eyes.'

She was beautifully fresh from her bath, naked skin glowing beneath the semi-transparent material of her robe. Rippling over her shoulders the long mane of hair gave her an appearance of unspoiled young innocence. She stood before Marlo, her perfume a seductive cloud. Lifting her arms she rested her hands on his shoulders and smiled into his face.

'I've missed you, darling,' she said.

Beneath the make-up he felt himself begin to sweat.

'Did they have to take my lovely boy away,' she crooned. 'Operate on his poor head so as to remove that nasty spare part.' Her fingers caressed the top of his skull, slipped over his shoulder, dug nails into the flesh of his back.

'Darling,' he said in a soft, low, husky whisper. 'I love you, my darling. I need you. I long to possess your body.' He wasn't pretending. If she wanted to play the instant-aphrodisiac the dentist had fitted in a tooth dispenser wouldn't be needed.

Nails dug again into his flesh. Bleakly he tongued the anti-passion dope also fitted as part of the service. Damn the girl! What was she playing at?

'There's no time for games now, precious,' she murmured softly, running her hands over his bare torso. 'Undress and go to bed now.'

Obediently he stepped towards the bed, dropped the loincloth Quail had draped about his lower regions, and climbed between the sheets. His head pounded like a drum and the inside of his mouth was dry. Every natural instinct was screaming out for him to reach out and grab the girl and to hell with everything else. He bit down on the inside of his cheek and tasted blood as he fought for control. The doorchime came to the rescue.

It was the guard making his last personal check of the day. Marlo took the opportunity to relax a little. The timing had been just right. Now there would be all night to operate without interruption. By a tremendous effort of will he managed not to look at her as she dropped her robe and slipped naked into the bed.

Nails dug into his back as she played with her toy.

'Talk to me,' she commanded. 'Darling, talk to me!'

Marlo punched her scientifically beneath the chin.

A hundred and twenty-three two millimetre pills don't take up much room but they aren't invisible. They have mass, bulk, a distinct colour. They were soluble and would be in a container of sorts. Finding them could only be a matter of time.

Marlo checked the girl to make sure that she was both unconscious and comfortable. A third container in his mouth yielded an anaesthetic gas that would keep her quiet for fifteen minutes at a time. Before she woke he would lie down beside her unresponsive to her commands. The punch would have been the last act of a failing mechanism. She would call Quail who would make the exchange carrying Marlo and the pills right out of the apartment under her very nose.

Simple.

Only he couldn't find the pills.

He went through the bathroom with a fine comb and drew a blank. Back in the bedroom he frowned, thinking. The apartment wasn't large. It had a bathroom, bedroom, kitchen and living room. The furniture was supplied together with the fittings. Naomi had brought little with her. A couple of cases with some clothes and other stuff aside from the mannikin. He checked the time and fed her another shot of gas.

The girl was a paranoiac. She would need to have the stuff close to her and, from what he could see, she spent most of the time in bed.

He found a mass of frilly underthings, a complete range of cosmetics, a stilleto, a small automatic pistol, a gas pencil, an anti-rape defence mechanism and a ring that squirted corrosive fluid. The wardrobe held street clothes and a folding container for the mannikin. There was also a man's suit together with shoes and underwear. Her fantasy had obviously included dressing up her toy as the occasion demanded.

Back in the living room he fought against the conviction that he was running out of time. The walls were of solid concrete without the trace of a crack. The seats and cushions were covered with tough plastic that showed no sign of break or tear. The furniture was made of steel tubing, the ends welded tight. Fuming he rolled back the carpet figuring that, maybe, she had spread out the pills between layers of plastic film.

Nothing.

The kitchen yielded another blank. He checked the time and stormed back into the bedroom. Halfway to the door the phone rang. Marlo ignored it, entered the room and grabbed Naomi as she snatched up the pistol.

'Drop it!' He shook it from her hand. Her eyes were wide, still vacuous from the effects of the gas. 'I've drawn the teeth of all your toys,' he said. 'Don't waste time trying to kill me.'

'Quail,' she said thickly. 'I'll kill him for this!'

She was smart and he regretted the gas had failed to keep her under. His own fault, he had stretched the time too fine; but her waking had put him in a spot. He spoke quickly before her gas-lethargy could give way to panic-hysteria.

'Relax. I don't want to hurt you. Your old man hired me to get what you took from the plant. Just give me the stuff, and I'll be on my way.'

She snapped at his throat, her teeth nipping his skin before he could push her away, hands conscious of her nudity. He threw her back on the bed, flung a robe after her.

'Get dressed.'

She looked up, eyes calculating. 'Why? Don't you like me?'

'Sure I like you. Too much for my own peace of mind,' he said honestly. 'But what's that got to do with it? Where's the stuff?' He saw the muscles tighten along the line of her jaw. 'Look,' he said, sitting beside her. 'Let's be sensible about this. The game's over and you've lost.'

He caught her fingers as they thrust at his eyes. Her knee lifted, reached for his groin but missed because of their awkward position. He swore as the top of her head butted him in the face. Violence aroused desire. He flung her away and rose from the bed. To yield to temptation now was to commit suicide.

'You're crazy!' Marlo wiped blood from his nose. 'Do you want to die for the sake of a few lousy pills?'

'You get them you'll kill me,' she said. 'Right?'

'Wrong.' Irritably he pulled at the surrogate flesh plastering his face. Sweat had weakened the bond. It pulled free in curling strips. He tore at his scalp wishing that he could use alcohol, soap and a stiff brush but not daring to leave the woman alone. One call and the place would be stiff with guards. 'Those pills,' he said. 'Just how important are they?'

'If you don't know then I'm not telling you.' She lit a cigarette and stared at him quizzically through the smoke. 'You know,' she said, 'you're quite handsome in a savage kind of way.'

'Let's keep to the point.'

'I am.' She blew more smoke. 'You're in a spot and we both know it. I'm the only one who can get you out of here alive. If you kill me then you're a dead duck. If you hurt me the same.' She smiled. 'You know what? You've got a tiger by the tail.'

Marlo scowled. What she said was true enough but he didn't have to like it. He didn't have to admit it either. Not if he hoped to stay alive.

He dressed, led the way into the living room, poured them both drinks. The phone rang as she took her glass. A spiritual teacher was offering his services. They both ignored the instrument. Marlo helped himself to one of the cigarettes. 'This,' he said casually, 'is an interesting situation.'

She smiled. 'It's an impasse.'

'Not exactly. Let's review it. If I kill you the guards will kill me. If I don't kill you then you will order the guards to kill me. I may not have any option but you have. You've got the choice between living and dying.'

Her smile wavered a little. 'You wouldn't kill me.'

'If you believed that you wouldn't be talking,' said Marlo. 'You'd be calling the guards.' Anger roughened his voice. 'Of course I'd kill you, why not? I'm hoping that you won't make me do it.' He sipped his drink, watched as she tasted hers. 'Let's make a deal,' he suggested. 'Figure some way out of this mess.'

'You do the figuring,' she said. 'It's you who are on — '

The phone rang, interrupting her. Marlo grabbed her arm as she lunged towards the instrument, eyes narrowed as he read the displayed information.

The caller was Phillip Wayne of Chicago Chemicals. The face looked familiar. He had worn it himself. The mannikin still wore it.

Marlo held back the girl as she tried to reach the phone. 'No,' he said.

'But he's calling. I've got to answer.'

'Let him sweat.' Scowling he looked at the picture face. 'So that's it,' he said. 'You and he all the time.'

'Not quite,' she protested. 'Not as you think.'

'You worked together,' he insisted. 'You

88

must have been close.' His hand tightened on her wrist. 'Just what is this all about?'

He pushed her towards the bedroom, standing in the door, brooding, eyes dark with thought. More than ever he was conscious that time was running out. Wayne wouldn't give up trying to contact the girl. He would try again and, if there was no answer, he might alert the guards.

He tensed as the telephone rang. If it was Wayne!

It was a little old lady representing a charitable institution. She was obviously insane.

'All right,' said Marlo tightly. 'Talk — What is this all about?'

'Money,' she said. 'Power. Everything you've ever dreamed of.' She stepped towards him, smiling, as beautiful as sin. 'Real power. Power that would make you a king among men. A literal king!'

Marlo sneered. 'Words!'

'More than that,' she insisted. 'It's real. It's what you're looking for. Phillip discovered it. He's clever, dedicated. He has a dream and he's going to let me share it. Let me live and I'll share it with you. The three of us can rule the world!'

'The three of us?' Marlo raised his eyebrows. 'What about your father? Won't he want a share of the cake?'

'He can go to hell!'

'He probably will,' agreed Marlo. 'But Wayne works for Chicago Chemicals. He made the stuff in your old man's laboratory. Couldn't others figure out what he did?'

Naomi laughed. 'Phillip's no fool. He destroyed all his notes, dismantled all his apparatus. He got rid of his assistant and worked alone. He's got the secret locked in his head and no one can get it. If they try, if they hurt him — '

'You'll spread the discovery around,' interrupted Marlo. 'You'll pass the product to other chemical firms and they will learn the big secret. Smart,' he admitted. 'Phillip managed to get himself a load of insurance. A pity you haven't the same protection.'

'But I have,' she said quickly. 'I've got the tablets.'

'And if you get hurt what's your boy friend going to do — give away his big secret?' Marlo shrugged. 'If you believe that you've got space between the ears. All Phillip has done is to aim the heat in your direction instead of his. He's used you. Let me out of this trap and I'll prove it.'

She hesitated. 'No,' she decided. 'While I've got the pills I'm safe.'

'But you haven't got them,' said Marlo quickly. 'I have. At least I know exactly where they are.' And then, as her defences crumpled, 'Let's get out of here,' he said gently. 'Let's go home.'

★ ★ ★

Home was a nice place, warm with its facsimile fire burning against one wall and a facsimile window showing wind-swept rain lashing through bending trees to the muted appropriate sound-accompaniment. Marlo leaned back at his desk, listening to the small sounds coming from the kitchen still hardly able to believe his luck. Reaching out he adjusted a control. The window changed, showed the real weather outside, sleet carried on wings of darkness, ice and chill of approaching winter.

A lamp flashed on the desk. Marlo pressed a button, listened, spoke softly. 'Send him up.'

He rose, closed the door to the kitchen and returned to the desk. From a drawer he produced a phial containing one hundred and twenty-three lime-green pills. He was looking at them when the door opened and a man walked into the apartment.

'Mr. Wayne,' said Marlo. 'Make yourself right at home.'

'Where's Naomi?'

'A bad business,' said Marlo. 'The Staysafe Apartments didn't quite live up to their reputation. Still, there are compensations — even if you have lost your insurance.'

Wayne frowned. 'I don't know what you're talking about.'

Marlo looked up and smiled. The chemist looked pale, distraught. He kept both hands buried deep in the pockets of his overcoat.

'I think you do,' said Marlo quietly. 'And before we say anything more I'd appreciate it if you would put both your hands where I can see them.' He nodded as Wayne jerked out his hands. 'That's better. Some coffee?'

Wayne shook his head.

'Then let's talk.' Marlo picked up the phial of pills. 'You recognise these? You know, Naomi was an odd girl. She forgot that the obvious can sometimes be just that. She — '

'Was?' Wayne leaned forward. 'Is she dead?'

Marlo tossed the phial, caught it, tossed it again.

'So you killed her.' Wayne shrugged. 'Maybe it's just as well. A paranoiac like that can't be trusted. To hell with her.' His eyes followed the phial as Mario threw it into a drawer. 'How?'

'Simple. I was with Naomi when you phoned,' explained Marlo. 'As soon as I saw your face I knew where they must be. In her mannikin. The facsimile of you she'd had made to give her what you never could.' He looked at the chemist. 'Didn't you know she loved you?'

'Sure I knew. Who better? I made her feel that way. I'm a chemist, remember? A few shots of this and wiffs of that and she fell like an overripe mango. Of course it wasn't really love just a biological reaction, but how was she to tell the difference?'

'She admired you,' said Marlo softly. 'She trusted you.'

'Then she was a fool.' Wayne was contemptuous. 'In this world it's every man for himself and to hell with the rest. Start trusting someone and you put their hands around your throat.' He looked curiously at Marlo. 'You said that you were in her apartment. How did you get out?'

'It was simple,' said Marlo blandly. 'Naomi cleared me with the guards. That was before she — changed.'

'You killed her,' said Wayne. 'Why be prissy about it? You're an assassin, aren't you? A man for hire to take care of trouble.' He dismissed the subject. 'Those pills, how much do you want for them?'

'One half of the world.'

'I'm serious.'

'So am I.' Marlo leaned forward a little. 'That's what they're worth, aren't they?

Naomi thought so. She said they spelt absolute power. Was she crazy?'

Wayne breathed deeply, the air hissing through his nostrils. 'She wasn't crazy,' he said at last. 'Can you guess what those pills do? They re-establish the censor, that's what. You know what happens then?'

'Yes,' said Marlo.

'Slavery,' said Wayne. 'Total and abject slavery. The rule of fear for everyone except us!'

Something fell in the kitchen. There was a clatter and sounds of a female voice raised in anger. Wayne looked towards the closed door, stared at Marlo. 'Naomi,' he said. 'She's alive!'

'That's right,' said Marlo.

'But you told me that she was dead. That you'd killed her.'

'No,' said Marlo. 'I just let you think that. I wanted to get what you thought of her down on tape,' he explained. 'The way you felt. I don't want my wife dreaming of another man.'

'You married her? That paranoiac!'

'She isn't all that unusual,' said Marlo

slowly. 'Rich, envied, afraid that everyone she meets is after what she owns. Her trouble is that she needs someone to give her security. A sense of being wanted, of being special to someone.'

'A product of our age,' said Wayne. 'We could change it you and I. With my discovery we could put things back as they were. A time when the rich were respected and feared. When authority was obeyed. When the ordinary people kept their place.'

'And,' said Marlo drily, 'when lawbreakers were punished.'

'Exactly.'

'And who is to determine the law? Us?'

'Naturally.'

'And the same old cycle starts all over again.' Marlo shook his head. 'I prefer things as they are. Now we have no jails, no criminals, and courts, and no crime. Why? Because we have no law. A man has to protect what he owns — not expect others to do it for him.'

'A jungle,' said Wayne. 'That's what we're living in. A jungle.'

'We always have,' said Marlo. 'You

should study history. Can you guess how many were slaughtered on the road each year? How many were attacked, beaten, robbed, raped, killed and maimed for life by thugs and villains? How much each working person had to pay in taxes simply to support an organisation dedicated to keeping them in line? Do you realise they even had a law saying it was illegal not to know the law — that ignorance was no excuse? Can you guess how many laws there were? That it was literally impossible for anyone to go through life without breaking some, enforced or not. Don't talk to me about a jungle.'

'They had respect in those days. Respect for authority.'

Marlo flared. 'And why the hell should they have had? What did authority ever do for them? It kept them poor, kept them under. To hell with authority. This is a free world and I want it kept that way.'

'So that you can go around killing? A man with a gun and no brain? Someone who shoots down others for pay? For that what you call living in a free world?'

'It's better than what we used to have,'

said Mario coldly. 'So a few mothers kill their babies because they run out of patience, but is that anything new? Is assassination? Is taking things you want without asking? Making a grab at a good-looking girl? Lifting a fist to someone who steps on your toes?' Irritably he shook his head. 'Forget it, Wayne. This is my world and I like it.'

'And that's good enough for you,' said Wayne. 'Have you ever thought why things are as they are?'

'Some bug,' said Marlo. 'Some virus that escaped from some laboratory. Or maybe they let off one bomb too many. Who gives a damn now? The censor lost its power to restrain the impulse to action. And,' he ended, 'the society it fashioned went with it.'

Wayne shrugged. 'It'll come back,' he said. 'Better than before because the right people will be running it.'

'You?'

'Why not?' Wayne shrugged again and a gun fell from his sleeve into his hand. 'All right,' he said softly. 'Pass me the tablets.'

Marlo hesitated.

'Do it. Before I shoot your head off.'

Marlo reached into the drawer. The pills were imitation, the genuine ones he'd washed down the sink but while Wayne lived no one could wash the information from his brain. His hand fell on the gun he'd planted. He fired as the chemist moved forward, the heavy bullet hitting below the chin, travelling upwards to tear out the side of the face, the top of the skull.

The sound of the shot was enough to wake the dead.

To bury forever a bad, old world.

AGENT

I don't envy Looie.

I'd like his money and I could use his car but I can do without his fat, his bad heart and his reputation. Especially his reputation. It stinks.

In a profession abounding with lice he was the biggest louse of them all. A modern parasite leeching his twenty, thirty, even fifty percent as a so-called 'agent,' he was hated by everyone from the regular ten percenters down to the lowest chorine who ever kicked a leg before the footlights.

I worked for him.

He told me once that it gave him a lift to have a man with a college education around, especially if that man had been in the front line of the football team and, as he was willing to pay for what he wanted, I didn't find it too hard to take his cash. But I didn't have to like him.

I was sitting in the outer office when

the two men walked in. They looked odd but that was nothing. Most of the characters who wanted to see Looie looked odd. If they had been normal they wouldn't have wanted to see him in the first place. I put on my office expression as they halted before my desk.

'Mr. Samuels?'

'Who?' It took me a second to remember that Looie had been christened with his father's name. 'You mean Looie?'

'I mean Mr. Lewis Samuels.' The speaker, a tall, thin, pale-faced man looked at a card he held in his hand. 'I understand that this is his place of business?'

'That's right.' I reached forward and took the card from him. It was dirty, creased, and bore an almost indecipherable scrawl on the back. I nodded when I read it. 'If you will wait a minute?'

I rose before he could answer and passed into the inner office. Looie looked up as I entered. As usual he was eating, he always was — nuts, chocolates, cookies, the man had an appetite like the hog he was. I threw the card onto his desk.

'Customers. Willie sent them.'

'Willie?' He blew out a mouthful of crumbs and picked up the card. 'He still around?'

'They must have let him out a week ago.' Willie was a tout, a hanger-on at the racetracks, the bars, the pool rooms. A self-employed in-between man who drew a small commission from any business he sent our way. 'You want to see them?'

'Wait.' Looie frowned down at the card. 'Better be careful. Check with Willie, this may be a trap.'

I nodded and reached for the phone.

It took five calls and a lot of persuasion to contact the tout but I finally found him. He snapped into the phone as though I'd woken him up, which I probably had.

'Yeah?'

'Willie? Sam here. A couple of characters just walked in with a card coming from you. Know them?'

'Two men? Tall? Skinny? Sound like foreigners?'

'That's right.'

'I know them. Gave 'em the card last night. They wanted a flesh peddler.'

'A what!'

'You heard me. They want to buy some bodies.' Willie chuckled. 'What's the matter, Sam? Looie getting touchy over what they call him?'

'No.' I knew that in Willie's parlance a flesh peddler was anyone who dealt in human talent. 'Just wanted to check up. Looie thinks that it might be a trap.'

'How can it? I only did a month in the pen, never mind for what, but that was out of town.' His voice grew hungry. 'Say, Sam, any chance of a touch? Those two guys are good business and I need some dough.'

'I'll get in touch with you.' I set down the receiver and nodded to Looie. 'Willie says that they're O.K. Bring them in?'

Looie nodded.

They came straight to the point.

'We are interested in buying some humans,' said the one who had spoken to me in the outer office. 'I understand that you are in business to supply what we want.'

It was a bit raw, even for Looie. He glanced towards me where I sat in a corner, just in case, then pursed his lips.

'I can supply talent,' he admitted. 'What did you have in mind? Hoofers? Canaries? Skin beaters?'

'Men and women.'

'I know, but for what? Singers? Dancers? Musicians?' He frowned. 'You putting on a show, or something?'

The man who had spoken before hesitated then turned to his companion. They muttered for a while, something I couldn't catch, then the tall guy turned to face Looie again.

'You confound me. Do you sell men and women, or not?'

'Sure I sell 'em, their contracts that is, but what sort and how many?' Looie was getting impatient. 'You starting a road show? Night club? Do you want artistes for a spot south of the border?' He didn't leer as he said it but the hint was plain. 'I can fix you up with as many as you want.'

'A hundred? Two hundred?'

'As many as you want,' repeated Looie dully. He glanced towards me and I stepped forward. I guessed that he was out of his depth.

'Mr. Samuels will supply any number of artistes you may require,' I said. 'Just tell him how many and what you are thinking of paying.'

'Pay,' said the man. He turned to his companion and muttered again. 'We will pay one thousand dollars per head.' He fumbled in his pockets. 'Here.'

I've heard tales of the old currency, I've even seen it in museums, but I never thought that I'd live to see a shower of gold scattered over a desk in a modern office. The coins made a lovely ringing sound as they fell, one or two of them rolling to the floor. I stooped and picked them up. They were gold all right. Double Eagles, Sovereigns, Escutadoes. Pieces of Eight. Golden Louis. I let them trickle through my hands in a gleaming shower.

'There is one thousand dollars in gold,' said the stranger. 'It is yours. I will pay you one thousand dollars for every man and woman you supply.'

'Leave it with me,' said Looie hastily. His fingers closed over the golden heap. 'Come back tomorrow, same time, I'll have an answer for you by then.'

'Tomorrow,' said the man. He hesitated. 'There are other things. You can supply them?'

'Sure.' Looie didn't ask what. He was too intent on the gold.

After they had gone we counted the gold. I didn't know just how much there was, it would take an expert to value the coins, but in sheer weight the stuff came to well over a thousand dollars. Looie pursed his lips as he stacked the coins. 'What do you think, Sam?'

'I don't like it.' I reached for a sovereign. 'There's something fishy going on. Normal people wouldn't pay their bills in gold, not when it's worth several times its face value. And the way that man spoke! He talked of men and women as though they were cattle.'

Looie shrugged. He spoke about them the same way, probably thought of them like that too. 'So what? If he's willing to pay a thousand dollars a head in this sort of stuff . . . ' His voice trailed off as he reckoned his immediate profit. 'Say it's just worth double. Two thousand dollars plus twenty percent, no thirty, of all wages. Two hundred people.' He whistled.

'Grab ten off the books, for starters, Sam. Pick lookers. Young, hungry, and not too particular. I want to get on this gravy train.'

'But what does he want them for?'

'How the hell do I know?' Looie snatched the sovereign from my hand. 'Get busy!'

It wasn't hard to find ten chorines willing to work, place unknown. By the time the two men came back I had them lined up for inspection, contracts signed with a space left blank for the salary but with thirty percent of whatever it was scheduled for Looie's pockets.

The men didn't even look at them. They walked into the inner office and, after a while, Looie sent for me. I was curious, I'll admit it, and took a good look at them as I passed. Looie gestured with his hand.

'My assistant. He will fix up whatever you need.'

'Will I?' I stared at the strangers. 'What do you want?'

'A place where we can process the people you have sold to us.' As before the man's voice was flat, stilted, utterly devoid of emotion. The way he said the words made me think of a foreigner. 'We have certain machinery and we need somewhere large to set it up.'

'Rehearse them, you mean?' I frowned. 'There's the old theatre at the edge of town. It's been shut for the past ten years but I could get it for you.'

'What about the warehouse down on Seventh-street?' Looie owned the warehouse and I could guess what he was after. 'You could rent that for them. It wouldn't cost much to fix a stage and it's wired for power.' He looked at the strangers. 'That do?'

'Is it large?'

'Big enough to train a regiment.'

They muttered together again, a hissing rush of sibilants, then the spokesman nodded. 'It will do. You have the people?'

'Outside.' I jerked my thumb towards the door. 'Shall I tell them to report to the warehouse?'

'Tomorrow. You will show us the place?'

'We'll have you fixed up inside a day.' Looie reached for the phone. 'That's all, Sam. You know what to do.'

★ ★ ★

Things moved fast after that. The first ten chorines went to the warehouse and that was the last I ever saw of them. More followed, lots more, and men too. At first I tried to pick those with some genuine talent then, as Looie began to get more greedy and as the strangers didn't complain, we skimmed the books for all the broken down hams, the so-called comics, the dancers who had long forgotten their prime, the musicians with ten thumbs instead of fingers, the dregs and fringes of an overcrowded profession.

Each one we sent was paid for in gold and Looie seemed to get fatter and greasier every day. He was satisfied, why shouldn't he have been? But me? I was getting worried.

Little things started it. The utter impartiality of age or sex, talent or lack of skill of the people we sent them. The way the warehouse seemed to swallow them up without trace. The steady, incredible stream of gold that found its way into Looie's hands.

I wondered about that gold. I asked questions at the museums and from noted experts in numismatics. I even stole a piece I found lying in a corner and had it analyzed. The gold was there, all right, the trouble was that there was too much of it. The assay showed at least fifty per cent of the precious metal. The coins were, as I suspected, counterfeit.

The whole thing didn't make sense.

The blow-up came when we had a visitor from the Health Department. He didn't waste any time with me but went straight in to Looie. I followed him as a matter of course, Looie was the sort of man to attract violence, and anyway, I was curious. The inspector came straight to the point.

'You own that warehouse down on Seventh-street?'

'Yes,' said Looie cautiously. 'Why?'

'It stinks. We've had complaints from the neighbours and you've got to clean it up.' He stared at the fat man. 'What are you running it as, anyway? A slaughter-house?'

'That's ridiculous.'

'Is it? Well it smells that way to me. Who's working there now?'

'Some people hired it from me,' said Looie quickly. 'I don't know what they wanted it for, experiments I think. Why don't you ask them?'

'The place is locked.' The inspector stared his dislike. 'As you're the owner it's up to you to stop the nuisance. Better get working on it, if you don't stop it we will and fine you into the bargain.'

After he had left I sat on the edge of the desk and stared at Looie.

'Well?'

'Well what?'

'I had a feeling about those two men.' I told him about the coin assay. 'Now there are complaints of a funny smell down where they are working. If you ask me you're in trouble.'

'Why? Where's the harm in a new theatrical company rehearsing in a warehouse?'

'Rehearsing?' I shrugged. 'You can't believe that. We've sent them about two hundred men and women, all the drifters and hams in the business, and they still want more. Any legitimate producer

114

would have screamed for his money back at the talent we've supplied. It would take a genius to get even a third-rate show out of them.' I stopped him speaking with a stab of my finger. 'Don't mention South America. I could swallow that for a few girls, yes, but not for those grandmothers, charwomen, and shapeless morons we've been supplying. And what of the men? Do they want to ship them south too?'

'They know their own business,' Looie protested. 'I'm just an agent.'

'You're just a flesh peddler,' I agreed. 'That's what everyone calls you and . . . ' I stared at him. 'Say! Those men never said that they were going to rehearse. They spoke of processing the people we sent.'

'Slang.' Looie dismissed it with a wave of his pudgy hand. 'They're foreigners and don't know our terms.' He chuckled. 'They even said they'd pay so much a head. A head! Who the hell would want to buy heads?'

'Headhunters,' I said, and somehow it didn't seem funny. 'Looie! Suppose that they were speaking the literal truth? Suppose that they really did think you were a flesh peddler, that you could sell men and women? Remember how they asked you to sell them humans? Remember how they never took off their hats or coats, even though it's June? And they paid you in gold at so much a head. And they processed the people we sent them. And now the Health Department is complaining about the smell.'

'Sewers,' Looie said. 'That warehouse was condemned a long time ago.' He reached for a bowl of nuts. 'Quit worrying. You talk as though those two men were Martians or something.'

'Maybe they were.' I swallowed as I thought about it. 'Or time travellers, or robots, or anything you like to pick. They counterfeited gold coins, maybe they wanted to make sure that they had a currency good for any era. They wanted heads, and Willie sent them to you telling them that you sold flesh. How the hell would they know about slang? They must have taken him at his word.'

'You're crazy,' said Looie, but I could see he was shaken. 'They're human, why should they want heads?'

'Does it matter? Suppose that we wanted something from the past. Neanderthal skins for example. We went back and found someone who said that he could sell them to us. Would we consider them human? We'd take what was offered.' I snapped my fingers. 'Perhaps they were traders from another planet or dimension or time. They wanted heads, brains rather, perhaps for study, perhaps for use. You told them you could supply them with what they asked for. You took their money and sent them people.' I rose from the edge of the desk. 'I'm going down to the warehouse and find out what's going on.'

★   ★   ★

The place was silent when I got there. I discovered what the Health Department was complaining about straight away. The smell was sickening, the only thing like it I've ever experienced was once when I lived near a fertilizer plant.

Lighting a cigarette I managed to break in and take a look around.

117

No strangers. No machines. No signs of life. At one end of the place I found signs that seemed to show some electrical equipment had been used, scraps of wire and insulation. The dust was scuffed and disturbed by footprints and, in a small office-like room, I found the thing that sent me streaking out of the building towards the nearest phone. I found something else too, but I don't like to think of that.

The office contained two bodies. Two men, tall, thin, pale-faced men. Only they weren't bodies. They were like dummies, built of plastic and wire. They were empty and I mean that literally. Two hollow shells that had once contained — what?

The other thing was what made me retch and retch and keep on retching.

We had sent two hundred men and women down to the warehouse and they were still there. But not all of them. Each one had lost something vitally important. In the warehouse rested two hundred neatly decapitated corpses.

As I said, I don't envy Looie!

THE INEVITABLE
CONFLICT

1

It looked like a tiny speck against the clear blue of the sky, an insect, a minute point of black high in the heavens. It seemed to hover for a moment, poised beside the towering wall of the high building, then, with shocking abruptness, it expanded, grew, took on a recognizable form.

Arms sprouted from it, legs, the blob of a face and the streaming, wind-whipped garments of a man. It twisted a little as it fell and from it came a thin, high-pitched screaming. It struck, smashing against the concrete of the sidewalk with a horrible soggy sound and, from it, blood plumed in a fine red rain.

Curt Harris had been too close.

He had almost been crushed, the passage of the body throwing him to one side; now, having regained his feet, he stood, muscles trembling with the reaction of his narrow escape, and dabbed stupidly at the blood on his light clothing.

He glanced at the messy, bloodstained pulp lying almost at his feet, then gulped and looked away.

Around both he and the dead man a crowd had gathered, pressing forward and staring with the peculiar morbidity common to crowds at the broken remnants of what had once been a man.

'You there! What happened?' The police officer thrust himself forward, driving through the crowd with practiced ease.

'A man jumped off the roof.' Curt dabbed at his ruined suit then, as he only managed to smear the blood even further over the thin material, gave up the futile task. 'I watched him fall. He came from this building and almost hit me when he landed.'

'Tough luck.' The officer was casual in his sympathy. He activated his radio and muttered into his throat mike, glancing at the chronometer on his wrist and squinting up at the building. He stared at Curt. 'You look as if you had one a hell of a shock.'

'I have. All right to leave?'

'Sure. The guy's dead and I guess you

couldn't have pushed him.' The officer attended to his radio then yelled at the crowd. 'All right! Be on your way! The show's over!'

Curt dabbed at his face with a clean handkerchief he had taken from an inner pocket. It was of little use and he stared at the soiled fabric in disgust then, crumpling it into a ball, threw it beside the corpse.

'You going in there? The Interplanet Building?' The officer nodded towards it.

'That's right.'

'Maybe you should get cleaned up first. There is a sauna way down the road. They could even do something about your suit.'

'Thanks for the suggestion,' said Curt dryly. He stared up at the tall building, then, glancing down at his clothes, hesitated. He looked a mess, the blood made ugly blotches against the light material and from the stiffness of his features he could imagine what he must look like.

But he was late, in a temper, his nerves jangled from shock and reaction. Determined, identification in hand, he strode towards the wide doors.

The receptionist was young, sleek, a product of accepted fashion. Her hair a shimmering blonde cascade, face masked in cosmetics, nails a vivid emerald, clothing skillfully accentuating her femininity. She lifted her head as Curt strode towards her and stared at him with undisguised hostility.

'Yes?'

'My name is Harris. I have an appointment.'

'Indeed? With whom?'

'With your boss. He sent for me.' He fumbled in his pocket and produced an envelope. 'Here. Maybe you can make out the details. I need a wash. Where can I find the men's room?'

It was clean and bright and comforting as everything else would be in this place. The attendant was helpful, trying to mask his curiosity as he provided an extra towel and did his best to sponge the stains from the jacket and shirt.

'This won't be easy, sir.'

'Never mind, just do your best.'

'A confrontation?'

'Something like that.'

Curt dipped his head into the water to end the discussion. He washed, laving his flesh to cleanse it of blood and sweat, soaping face, neck, shoulders and upper torso. He rinsed and refilled the bowl, the attendant discretely adding a touch of masculine perfume. Cleaned, dried, he straightened and, in the mirror, looked at his thirty-three-year-old face.

It was strong, smooth, with thick dark hair and grey eyes, both face and body tinted with a golden, permanent tan. Curt Alain Harris, an expert in the field of socio-biological engineering. A graduate from Harvard. A professor. One late of Venus. One almost late of Earth.

The receptionist greeted him with a smile and a look of frank admiration despite the stains on his suit.

'This is from the Director himself, sir.' She waved the envelope he had given her. 'Please give me a moment.' She tapped the keys of a computer and studied the screen. 'Your appointment is verified. The Director is waiting for you. Cybele will escort you to his office.'

She was almost as decorative as the receptionist, as the soaring columns, the arches, the carefully constructed make-believe of the interior of the building. Harsh, functional design had long been abandoned in favour of a more soothing environment but, despite her charm, Curt knew that she wasn't quite what she seemed. Young, attractive, charming with the lithe body of a dancer but, beneath the fabric of her clothing rested the muscles of a trained gymnast. One, he guessed, trained in the martial arts. One who carried emergency protection should he stray from the path, try to steal something, alter something, plant something in an inconspicuous corner. The thick bracelet she wore probably contained a stunning spray or anaesthetic darts.

Trust was at a premium in the Interplanet building as it was in the entire edifice of the Interplanetary Development Corporation, but he didn't dwell on it. Nor on the chatter of his guide, concentrating instead on the murals depicting the domed cities on the moon, the diggings on Mars, the station on Venus.

'Here we are, sir.' Cybele halted before

a door. 'If you will give me a moment while I announce you?'

'Go ahead.'

Time for him to do what he had come to do if he was a criminal or an assassin or someone who intended harm. But time, also, for the hidden security cameras to monitor his every gesture. His every move. He did neither, standing where his guide had left him, waiting for the summons.

Director Eric Carter was twice Curt's age but didn't look it. His face was lined and his hair thinner than it had been despite the cosmetic medication he took as a matter of course for no executive could afford to look less than fit and hearty. The Director looked both. He also wielded more influence and power than any ancient monarch. A man of his time. One who had risen with the exploding interest in extraterrestrial exploration, forming combines, cartels, monopolies often in complete disregard of restrictive legislation. Using the complexities of the law to his own ends. Tying space travel into a mesh of dependant installations.

Manipulating the greed of investors to finance his aspirations.

He rose from behind a wide desk as Curt entered the room, smiling and extending a hand.

'Harris! Good of you to come.' He didn't seem to notice the other's dishevelled appearance. Curt shook the proffered hand and slumped into a chair facing the wide desk.

'Sorry I'm late,' he apologized. 'Some fool decided to jump off your roof just as I arrived.' He stared ruefully at his clothing. 'He missed me by a hair, but his blood gave me a shower bath. I would have changed but all my stuff is at the airport and it would have taken too long.'

'Someone jumped off the roof?' Carter frowned. 'Are you sure?'

'I watched him fall. It was from this building right enough. Probably a visitor. Some poor devil who decided to end it all.'

'No.' Carter was positive. 'It couldn't have been that. The roof is banned to the public and the upper floors are sealed.' He reached for the intercom on his desk. 'Medway?'

'Speaking.'

'Carter here. Someone has committed suicide. Jumped off the roof. Check all personnel and report back as soon as you discover who it is.'

'Yes, sir.'

Carter sighed and relaxed in his padded chair, his broad features relaxed and giving him the appearance of a dreaming idol. 'I'm sorry about what happened. It was a hell of a welcome. Did you make a note of the time?'

'No. Why?'

'It might have helped.' Carter didn't elaborate his ambiguous remark. 'Did you have a good journey?'

'Not too bad. One of the jet engines cut out shortly after we left England but that was all.'

'I see. You didn't note the time it cut did you?'

'No. Should I have done?'

'It doesn't matter. The details will be in record and can be checked.' Carter hit a button as the intercom hummed its attention signal. 'Yes?'

'Medway here, sir. Personnel check

complete. Benwick is missing.'

'Benwick?' Carter's voice rose in sudden anger. 'Damn it, Medway! I warned you to be careful!'

'I know and I did my best. He must have wandered off and found an unlocked door to the roof. I'm sorry, sir.'

'Regrets won't bring him back. You should have been more careful.' Carter paused, frowning, his fingers drumming on the edge of his desk. 'Better get down here,' he snapped. 'Harris has arrived.'

The intercom died and the Director looked thoughtfully at Curt as if assessing his visitor. Evaluating him against potential stress.

'I'm sorry, Harris, but in a way you have arrived too late.'

'Too late? Too late for what? I don't understand.'

'No. Of course not. But you will. The pity of it is that the man who was to have explained it to you is dead. The one man you would have found most interesting has gone.'

'Benwick?'

'Yes. Professor Benwick. You know him?'

'No.' Mounting irritation finally reached its limit and Curt snapped, 'What's this all about? Why did you send for me? Why the desperate urgency?'

'Because the matter is urgent. To you, to me, to us all. Benwick was to have explained,' Carter said bitterly. 'He knew his danger and tried to guard against it. Obviously we underrated it, or perhaps nothing we could have done would have prevented it. I don't know.'

'Then . . . ?'

'Benwick is dead. A suicide. Killing himself by his own action, throwing himself off the roof to certain destruction. It could have been an accident but . . . ' The old man shook his head and Curt stared at him with growing impatience.

'But what? Get to the point.'

'Benwick is dead, Harris — and you almost died with him. That is the point.'

2

Medway was in his early fifties, tall and thin with a harassed expression and blond hair. He stared at Curt with washed-out blue eyes and his thin hand felt limp and a little clammy. Curt shook it, feeling as if he were holding a snake then, the polite formalities over, slumped back into his chair.

'A pity you arrived late, Harris.' Medway almost collapsed into a chair opposite, sighing as though he was on the verge of exhaustion. 'I'm sure you would have been interested in Benwick.'

'If I'd arrived a second earlier,' said Curt grimly, 'Benwick and I would have met — fatally.'

'Yes, Medway.' Carter leaned across his wide desk. 'What about that? How did he manage to commit suicide?'

The thin man shrugged.

'I don't know. He knew his danger as well as we, and he seemed determined

132

not to do anything foolish. I'd left him for a moment in order to bathe my eyes and when I returned he had gone.' He sighed again. 'Maybe I was careless,' he admitted. 'But I haven't slept well for days now and, anyway, how was I to know that someone had left the roof door open?'

'True.' Carter nodded and, for the first time, Curt realized that the old man, like Medway, was on the edge of physical exhaustion.

'Look,' he said, and sat up in his comfortable chair. 'I hate to remind you of this but I'm here because of an urgent appointment. One you arranged. Your summons interrupted my vacation in England. Would you mind telling me what all this is about?'

'I'm sorry, Harris, you must forgive me. Benwick's death has come as a shock. It shouldn't have happened. Tell him, Medway.'

'You didn't know Benwick. In a way there is no reason why you should, but you both had something in common, and it may have helped had you known him.'

'Well I didn't. What did we have in common?'

'You had both been to Venus.' Medway paused as if the statement was self-explanatory. Curt shrugged.

'So what? Were we the only ones?'

'No, but you and Benwick were the only two men still alive who had returned from Venus. Benwick returned about the time you landed. That was about a year ago wasn't it?'

'Not quite. I spent six months there and I've been back about four. Benwick must have left about a month before I landed. We probably crossed in transit.'

'Why did you go to Venus, Harris?'

'Don't you know?' Curt glanced at the Director. 'You people sent me. I did as you asked then came back here to finish my work on those Martian artifacts the Lamatre expedition found. I finished that project a few weeks ago and took off for a vacation. Your summons followed me to England and I caught the next stratoliner back. Surely you must know all this?'

'It would be in the files,' apologized the thin man. 'Personally we haven't much knowledge of you, the Greater New York office handles normal interplanetary traffic, we are mainly concerned with research.'

'So?'

'So we are worried, Harris. Not many men have returned from Venus as yet. Most of them are still working out their contract time. Some have returned, of course, thirty-seven to be exact, but . . .'

He paused and Curt shifted uneasily in the silence. 'But what?'

'But they are all dead. An hour ago only you and Benwick still remained alive out of the thirty-seven. Now Benwick is dead.' He stared at Curt. 'You are the only living man who has been to Venus. The only living man on Earth who has returned. And, if our predictions are correct, you are going to die at almost any moment.'

Curt Harris was no fool. No man who had spent half his life travelling and living in strange and alien places could be a fool — and live. He accepted what the thin man had said but, even as he accepted it, his mind was busy as it turned and worried at the information. He had a peculiar gift for deduction and extrapolation; the ability to take items of information, to probe them for validity and build from them to extend their area. To take facts and from them to build more.

He said, 'Let's get a few things straight. When you talk of men returning from Venus you aren't talking about those who handle the spaceships. You're talking about those contracted to work at the Station. Am I correct?'

'Naturally. I thought that was obvious?'

'Why?' Curt corrected the Director. 'It isn't obvious at all. We need to get this right. It's safe to call but not to stay. So time is an element. Disease?'

'No.' Medway shook his head. 'At least none that we can discover. If it were a disease it would be simple to handle. We could plot the incubation period, isolate the cause, determine the course of illness and, most probably, find a cure. No, Harris. It isn't disease.'

'Coincidence, then?'

'Thirty-six coincidences? Barely possible, perhaps, but we know it isn't coincidence.'

'Assassination?' Curt shrugged as he made the suggestion. 'Remote, I'll grant,

136

but still a possibility.'

'No.'

'Then I give up. You've had more time to work on the problem than I have. However, to me, it seems a simple one. You have thirty-six recorded deaths and each would have been investigated and so be accompanied by a mass of data. Out of all those facts you must have found some common factors. Surely it wouldn't be too difficult to sieve them, discard some, retain others? To me that would be obvious.'

'Yes,' said Medway, and fell silent. Carter cleared his throat with a rasping sound.

'You must not think we're all fools here, Harris. At first we didn't realize that anything was wrong. Men died, but men are always dying, there is nothing strange in that. It was only when we realized that the Venus-return death rate was so high as to be abnormal that we began to investigate. Soon we had only three remaining personnel left. You, Benwick and Lanson. We sent for you all.'

'Lanson died?'

137

'Yes. For some reason he stepped in front of a car. He died before he got here. We were luckier with Benwick, but he is dead, and now you are our only hope.'

Curt frowned. 'Lanson stepped in front of a car, you say? Are you trying to tell me that all of those thirty-six men committed suicide?'

'Suicide or accident.' Carter leaned across his desk. 'Silly accidents, stupid, utterly insane. One man squinted through the barrel of a shotgun, found it empty — and forgot the other was loaded. Another fell down three steps and broke his neck. One went fishing, caught a big one, and was pulled into the lake and drowned. They are the silly accidents I meant, but they are in the minority. The rest died by their own hands or, like Lanson, threw all elementary caution to the winds and paid the penalty.'

He looked hard at Curt.

'One thing is certain. Not one of those men died from natural causes. No disease. No organic failure. No illness or post operative relapse. Death, when it came, was quick and final.'

'And they had all returned from Venus. Had all worked at the Station?'

'Like you, Harris. Yes.'

'I see.' Curt leaned back in his chair and stared up at the ceiling. He was intrigued rather than worried. Thirty-six deaths out of all those dying every day wasn't many, and coincidence could play some peculiar tricks. Still it was peculiar that all the men who had returned from Venus should die. That was stretching coincidence too far. It hinted at some outside agency, some overall factor, something almost tangible that had threatened the men.

Carter's voice broke in on his thoughts.

'So you see, Harris, we are relying on you to help us. Obviously no more men can be bought back from Venus until we know what is causing these deaths. As you are the sole remaining man who has been there and returned we hope to find out from you what is the cause. Naturally, you will help us.'

'Will I?' Curt stared at the Director. 'What makes you say that?'

'Logic. Self-preservation. Thirty-seven

men have returned from Venus. Thirty-six of those are dead. Is there any reason to suppose that the entire thirty-seven will not die? You are the last, Harris. You're on a razor's edge. At this moment your life isn't worth a damned thing.'

'No?'

'No, and I can prove it.' Carter glanced at the thin man. 'I suggest we all go to the upper floor where there is something I want you to see. Medway, you will accompany us.'

'Must I?' The thin man was reluctant. 'I'm so tired. Can't it wait?'

'No. Tomorrow may be too late. Harris may be dead and our last hope gone.'

He rose and Medway rose with him. Curt remained seated.

'Please accompany us to the upper floor,' urged Carter. 'There is something I want you to see. Nothing startling, but I think you will find it most interesting. If you will be so kind?'

Curt shrugged and rose and followed the others towards the elevator.

3

The accident happened just as all accidents happen, unexpected, unpredictable and totally unguarded against. The signal lights over the elevator door flashed their message and the door slid open with a soft exhalation of compressed air. Curt stood a little ahead of the others and, as the door opened, he stepped forward his foot outstretched, his weight shifting to his unsupported leg. A reactionary gesture. One done innumerable times before by he and all others taking a single step. But this time was different.

There was no elevator, no cage, no floor to take the weight of his unsupported foot.

For the merest fraction of time he didn't realize what had happened then, as he felt himself beginning to fall down the shaft his hands clutched frantically at the edges of the door. For a moment he hung in awful suspension, his fingers slipping on the smooth plastic.

Frantically he glared into the shaft. The elevator was of the latest type without central cables and with a modular, self-motivated cage. There was nothing to offer a grip against his inevitable fall to the basement two thousand feet below.

In a matter of seconds he would end like Benwick.

Then hands clawed at him. Seizing his arms, his neck, grabbing at his hair. For a moment he tottered on the brink of eternity then, with agonizing slowness, Medway and the Director pulled him back to safety.

He grunted as he regained his balance and sagged against the wall, sweat standing in great beads on his forehead, and the cold shock of reaction tearing at his nerves. His hands trembled and he raised them, staring at the blood oozing from beneath his fingernails as if they belonged to someone else.

Staring as, in imagination, he was falling down the elevator shaft, spinning, aware, knowing what would happen when he reached the end, knowing it was inevitable that he would. Seeing again the mound of pulped flesh and shattered bone, the carmine hue of spouting blood. Seeing himself as he would be. As he would have been had he been alone.

'Harris?' Carter stood before him, breathing deeply, his face flushed, the veins prominent in his throat. His hand shook as he took a tablet from a foil packet in his hand. He thrust it into his mouth and handed the packet to Curt. 'Medication,' he explained. 'Take one. It will help to calm you down. Go on, you need it. Keep the packet. I've others.'

Drugs to aid the function of his heart, his lungs, certainly his nerves. A man of his age would need such help. Even so he was right. Curt needed it too. He shook out a tablet, chewed and swallowed it, thrust the packet into a pocket and waited until the sickness had faded and the fear and the trembling so that, he was able to climb the stairs after the others to the upper floor where Medway greeted him with a meaningful look.

'Thirty-seven,' he said significantly. 'You see what I mean?'

'That was an accident. How often does an elevator cage signal its arrival when it isn't there? A thing like that wouldn't happen once in a million times. Ten million.'

'Exactly.' Medway stared at the young man. 'And what is the probability factor against thirty-six men, all from the same place, all with diverse backgrounds, dying of suicide and freak accidents within one year of their arrival back home?'

'That's nothing to do with it.' Reaction-induced anger sharpened Curt's voice. 'The two things are totally different.'

'Are they?' Medway shrugged. 'Believe that if you want. Now we'd better hurry, the Director is waiting for us.'

Carter stood before a closed door. He seemed barely to have recovered from the recent ordeal despite his medication. He was impatient, snapping orders as they approached.

'Hurry, Medway. You know what you have to do.'

'I know.' The thin man fumbled in a pocket and produced a ring of keys. He unlocked the thick door, pushing it back on its slide then, as the others entered the room, closed it behind them.

Curt stared at what rested in the centre of the room.

It was nothing much, just a control panel, three chairs and a pair of elaborate headsets but around the construction quivered an aura of leashed power and, studying it, he gained the impression of a spider resting in its web. Interested he strode towards it.

'Careful,' warned Carter. 'Don't disturb the settings.'

'What is it?'

'A machine.' Carter seemed purposely vague. He stepped towards the control panel and studied the dials. Medway followed him, slipping into one of the chairs and staring distastefully at the headsets.

'I can see it's a machine.' Curt tried to control his impatience. 'I'm not a fool. What does it do?'

'Do?' Carter brushed the glistening panel with the tips of his fingers. 'It doesn't do anything but it offers the promise of a world. Do you know anything of cybernetics?'

'Naturally.'

'This is a cybernetic machine. It is the closest thing to a human brain mankind has ever built. This is just the control panel, of course, the main part of the machine is far below, well underground, shielded from any possibility of sabotage, accident and unwanted radiation.'

'I see.' Curt sat in one of the chairs. 'So, basically, it is a glorified adding machine.'

'No!' The old man was vehement. 'It's far from that. Think of the implications. You have a peculiar talent. You are able to extrapolate from given data and form conclusions that have a high degree of probability. It's that talent which has made you a valuable asset to the Interplanet Development Organization. The reason you were sent to Venus.'

'Well?'

'This machine does what you do but does it immeasurably better and with a probability factor which makes its findings as near to actual fact as can be desired. The theory has been known for a long time now and the motivation behind most of the electronic computers was to produce just such a machine. It remained impossible to do so, however, until we reached Venus.'

'How so?'

'The memory banks of all previous electronic machines were restricted to a limited versatility. The binary factor. That meant that literally millions of such units were required for even the simplest 'brain'. The tri-polar crystals from Venus solved that problem. They are capable of storing a fantastic amount of data and for the first time we really had a chance of building something which could approach the human brain.'

'So you have built a machine.' Curt was deliberately casual. 'What of it?'

Medway stirred in his chair.

'Think about it. We haven't just constructed an electronic device. We have built an infallible machine which is able to predict the future.'

'No.' Curt shook his head. 'What you have built is a machine able to assemble facts and from those facts to extrapolate something with a high degree of probability. There is nothing mysterious about that. It is merely basing a calculation on previous experience. If the sky is overcast, the air humid, the barometer falling, there is a high probability of storm. We know that. All your machine does is to add several more factors and from those extra facts deduce a higher degree of probability. When the storm will break, for example. How heavy will be the rain. How strong the wind. The duration, temperature and other things. All useful, I'll admit, but it has nothing to do with infallibility. It can do it because it has a larger memory and greater capacity for storing data than a human. But nothing is infallible. Nothing can ever be.'

'Perhaps not, but the Oracle is as close as anything could ever be.'

'The Oracle? Is that what you call it?'

'With reason.' Carter stared at the construct, a peculiar expression in his eyes. 'This machine isn't new. Its construction began shortly after men reached Venus, ten years ago now, and in all that time it has never been wrong. We have come to rely on it, to base our economy on it, to refer to it in case of doubt. We trust it,

Harris. We have to. No man or woman could ever plot the complexities of our civilization without such aid. There is too much to know, too many unrelated facts impinging one on the other, too many diverse fields of specialization. One wrong decision and Chaos could strike at any time.'

'You paint a dark picture.' Curt frowned at the control panel. 'But do you think it wise to rely on a machine?'

'Why not? At least it is unprejudiced and utterly logical.'

'So you say. But what has it to do with me?'

'It may mean your life,' said Carter quietly. He motioned towards Medway.

Silently the man reached for one of the headsets.

4

There was no sound. Nothing but subtle alterations in the glow of signal-lights on the control panel but Curt knew that far below something was stirring to strange and alien existence.

'There is a brief warm-up period,' explained Carter. 'We want to avoid any possibility of an overload. Medway?'

'Ready.'

'Commence the operation.' He paused, continuing as the other donned one of the headsets. 'We are using direct mental contact. Medway is letting the contents of his mind flow into the data banks below so as to update all available information. I am not sure if you are aware of the latest discoveries in paraphysical science but, in essence, we have found a means to project our thoughts. To transmit them, rather, from brain to machine. You are watching it happen.'

'It doesn't appear to be easy.' Curt

looked at the slumped figure of the thin man. 'Is that why he looks so fatigued?'

'Medway is a successful mutation. He has an eidetic memory but limited physical strength and staying power. He is also an electronic genius and had a great deal to do with the final formation of the machine. I think it possible they have formed some kind of affinity.'

'Isn't there danger in that? If a man projects his thoughts into the memory banks wouldn't he also project his emotions?'

'Perhaps, but the risk is one we have considered and decided to take. Medway is controlling that facet of his mind. He is concentrating on everything he knows concerning you. After he is through I want you to do the same. Then, with all available data fed into the memory banks the machine will be able to predict the time of your death. Hopefully it will also be able to give us the information we need to prevent the further waste of valued personnel.'

'Perhaps.' Curt stared at the console. 'One thing I don't understand. You told me that the machine has already predicted my death. Why, if you are already certain, are we going through all this?'

'The machine predicted the deaths of all who returned from Venus but, naturally, we had no chance to isolate the individuals concerned. Only Benwick and now you.'

'Benwick was tested?'

'Yes. Late last night.'

'And the prediction?'

Carter picked up a slip of paper from where it rested and handed it to Curt. He stared at it for a moment then read the typed words.

Prediction. Probability that subject will terminate within twelve hours. 99.99. Within nine hours. 99.54. Within six hours. 99.28. Probability that after termination of subject the sole remaining Venusian-return will die. Within twelve hours. 78.54. Within nine hours. 63.39. Within six hours. 54.32.

Curt stared at the Director.

'This was predicted by the machine?'

'Yes. Naturally we took stringent precautions. Benwick was never alone. He knew of the prediction and was determined to beat it. He lived ten hours.'

'Suicide!' Curt stared at the console, the paper crumpling in his hand. 'Why? What made him do it?'

'That is what we must discover. That is why I am hoping that you will be able to show us what it is that drove these men to their deaths.'

'At least he had a chance. His highest factor was 99.99 per cent. He still had a hope of beating whatever it was that killed him.' He remembered the wording of the prediction. 'Or terminated him. Why terminate? Doesn't the damn thing know the meaning of death?'

'99.99 per cent is the highest prediction the machine will ever make,' explained Carter. 'Did you notice your own figures?'

'Yes. High but I'm still alive.'

'And yet you have had two narrow escapes within the past hour. If the machine is correct, and I know that it is, your danger could increase. On the other hand it may not. That is what we need to know. Information that will help us. Something to give us a clue' He turned as

Medway removed the headset. 'We will soon know. Ready, Harris?'

'Forget it. I'm not going to put my head in that thing. Now don't get all upset. I refuse and that's final.'

'But why, man? Why?'

'I don't trust it. That's why.'

'Don't be a fool. How can it harm you?'

'I don't know,' admitted Curt, 'but I'm not taking any chances. If I'm slated to die then I don't want any machine to help me along the road. Benwick trusted you and Benwick is dead. Need I say more?'

'You stubborn idiot!' Carter blazed his anger. 'I thought you were an intelligent man. I'd hoped that you would be ready and willing to help us. The Oracle can't hurt you but the information it can yield could save the lives of those others on Venus. Isn't that worth a little inconvenience? Are we to abandon those men? Once the truth leaks out will they want to return home knowing they will die within a few months? Will others be willing to join them? Replace them? Do you realize just what is at stake?'

'Will my death help you?' Curt shook his head. 'You know it won't. I'm alive and I intend staying that way.'

'And I'm going to show you just how long you have.' Carter had mastered his anger. 'All right, Medway. It's useless to argue with him. Give the instruction.'

Tensely they waited as lights flashed on the console. Medway talking more to himself than to explain what was happening to the subject.

'The machine is scanning every item of information which could possibly have any bearing on your survival factor. It will take a few moments, incredibly fast though the relays are. Remember, it has to assess everything that has occurred up to this moment. When finished the code symbols are translated and typed. A copy is recorded on the instrument panel here. And, bear in mind, the machine is never wrong.'

He fell silent as a red lamp flashed. Carter withdrew a slip of paper from a slot, read it, handed it to Curt.

'What is it?' Medway was curious. 'What does it say?'

Curt ignored the man, concentrating on the few words typed on the paper.

Prediction. Probability that subject will terminate within twelve hours. 99.99. Within nine hours. 99.99. Within six hours. 99.99.

The paper crumpled as he clenched his fist in a savage determination to beat the message it carried. According to the prediction his death was certain within six hours, but never had he felt more vital, more fit, less ready for death.

It wasn't dying he was afraid of. Death was the one inevitable conflict no creature could avoid, but that was natural death not the cold, heartless calculations of an unfeeling machine.

He couldn't die within six hours! He couldn't! He wouldn't! And yet . . .

The machine was never wrong.

5

The sun was still warm when he left the building. On the sidewalk a dull stain marred the smooth surface, the sole trace of where a man had landed and dashed out his life in a spray of blood. Curt glanced at it then, his nerves and muscles tense with watchful caution, signalled to a passing cab.

'The airport,' he snapped to the driver. He grunted as the acceleration surge threw him back against the pneumatic cushions, then relaxed, his grey eyes clouding with thought.

Six hours.

Maybe less, he couldn't tell, it could be a matter of minutes but if the machine was right, and Carter had sworn it couldn't be wrong, he would be dead within six hours. Dead with the other thirty-six who had, like himself, returned from Venus. Dead like Benwick who had been warned, watched, protected and who had yet confirmed the prediction by his lethal jump.

Six hours — maximum!

For a moment panic gripped him and he leaned forward to tap the screen dividing him from the driver to order his return to the Interplanet Building and what safety it could provide.

'Yes?'

'Never mind.'

Curt forced himself to relax. There could be no safety back at the building, Benwick had proved that. Hiding was useless. Death wasn't something to be kept at bay with locked doors and sealed rooms. If he was to win this contest he had to depend on himself, not others, for this was a personal conflict. His life against — what?

What had killed the others? What thing had they bought back with them from Venus that had made them die?

He closed his eyes with a sudden weariness, throwing back his memories, trying to discover the one fact that could solve the problem. Save the lives of those yet to leave Venus but, above all, his own.

The cab slowed with a whine from its turbine. 'Airport, sir. Anywhere in particular? The locker luggage facility? Right.' Another few minutes and they had arrived.

'How much?' Curt counted out money when the driver told him and passed it into the man's hand through the opened port in the screen. As he left the taxi through the released door, he heard the driver's sudden yell.

'Hey! Not so fast! Look at you! What's that on your suit? Blood?'

'Paint.'

'Like hell it is.' The driver unlatched his own door and swung his legs towards the concrete. 'Stay where you are! The cops should get in on this!'

A shadow darkened the sky and instinctively Curt turned and began to run. He didn't look up. He didn't look back at the shouting driver. He bent his head and thrust his long legs against the concrete as he flung himself with frantic effort away from the thickening shadow.

Behind him came a scream and the rending of metal.

He stopped and turned. The taxi was a

heap of twisted metal and shattered crystal. A shattered wreck from which oozed a thin stream of blood. A wheel rested across it, one belonging to a stratoliner, and dimly he heard the shouts of others as they raced towards the scene.

He turned away. Another accident. Another million to one chance happening just when he would suffer from it. A wheel had fallen from a stratoliner, a thing which should have been impossible, but which had happened. Had he stayed to argue with the driver. If the man hadn't grown suspicious at the sight of the dried blood dappling his suit. If he hadn't been dictated by instinct to run he would be dead now like the hapless driver.

Mechanically he strode towards the lockers, claimed his luggage, hired a shower, bathed and changed. Emptying the pockets he threw the stained suit into the trash. Then, hunched over a cup of coffee, planned his next move.

Six hours!

He couldn't forget it. The machine had predicted that he would be dead within six hours. Predicted it with 99.99 per cent certainty. Not a hundred percent, but the machine couldn't predict absolute certainty. Always it had to allow for the unknown factor. In that he had been right. The machine was not infallible. If it was it wouldn't have left even that slender wisp of a hope.

He still had a chance.

The coffee was hot and he savoured it, feeling it warm his stomach and ease the tension of his nerves. Somehow he felt that if he could live through the next twelve hours he would be safe. Even the next six but it was better to play it safe. If the prediction could fail in one instance it could fail again and, if it did, he could be home and dry.

A game. He had to think of it as a game. A challenge similar to chess. His wits against the manipulations of the Oracle. If it was manipulating. If, somehow, it had gained the ability to affect data instead of simply recording it. Speculation which had no place. Now every effort had to concentrate on one thing. His personal survival.

But where to go to be safe?

The library was cool and restful the last place one would associate with violence and the scene of unpredictable accidents. The woman behind the desk was middle aged, somewhat plain, her clothing functional rather than decorative. Papers were scattered before her, lists, records, available material. A single flower stood in a vase. A plaque yielded her name.

Curt smiled as he used it.

'Lucy Weston?'

'Yes.'

'I'm a stranger and wonder if you could help me. I need to find somewhere secluded in order to study some specific material.'

'We have private cubicles for which there is a fee and the public rooms for which there is no charge. If you choose a cubicle the fee is payable in advance. How long would you require it?'

'That depends on how fast I can find out what I need to know. Maybe six hours?'

'Sorry. Only three are available before closing. You'll take them? Good. You are accustomed to the net, of course. Thank you.' She accepted his money and handed him back a stamped ticket. 'Cubicle seven. If you have trouble help can be supplied.'

The place was as he'd expected, small, a computer on a desk, a light, a chair. A curtain could be closed to mask the entrance and yield a measure of privacy. Curt wasted no time. The monitor glowed as he switched on the machine, icons dancing as he searched for appropriate sites, wishing, not for the first time, that things could be as simple as they once had before electronic magic had made books almost obsolete.

He was lucky, tracing the material he wanted without too much chasing around. Works on the paraphysical, genetic mutations, near-alien abilities, natural oddities, freakish happenings and, finally, what he hoped could be the answer. A book with an odd title. He frowned as he read it.

Accident Prones. A report on unpredictable accidents together with associated, open-thought speculations.

The author was someone he had never

heard of. A doctor with a string of initials after his name.

Curt settled himself on the chair and began to read. He had the ability to read quickly, a knack developed during his student days, but even so it took longer than he'd thought. He printed out the hard copy of the book title, author and publisher, then sat staring at the screen. He felt a little bemused, almost at a loss, but convinced he had found something new and of possible help.

The book was based on the statistical results of a host of insurance company records and it proved, beyond any reasonable doubt, that such things as accident prones really did exist. They were people whose mere presence caused accidents to happen. Why, no one knew. They were guiltless, personally not responsible for what happened around them, but their very presence ensured that the accident rate of the locale would increase.

It was a fact that had long been known and the author had followed several case histories, plotting each accident, the death rate, the monetary damage and the effect on the unfortunate prones. Not that they suffered, the accidents happened around them, not to them, but the insurance companies learned of them, refused to insure them, stepped up the rates wherever they were employed and, in general, made their lives a misery.

Curt mentally made connections. The Oracle had predicted his death within a certain period. Could it have determined that he was an accident prone? The suggestion was fantastic and yet it could hold the germ of an answer.

He rose and, leaving the cubicle, headed for the desk.

'Please,' he said to the librarian. 'I need to get in touch with the author of this book.' He showed her the printout. 'Doctor Jack Fenshaw. I've tried making contact but can't seem to manage it. Could you possibly help me?' He added, as she hesitated. 'It really is a matter of urgency. Do you have a registry?'

'Yes, sir, but you won't need it.' She smiled at his blank expression. 'If you want to contact Doctor Fenshaw I can help you. He lives in the city and is quite well known here.'

'Are you friends?'

'In a way. We talk a little when he comes.'

'Good.' His relief must have been obvious. 'Will you be so kind as to ask him to meet me here as soon as possible?'

'To meet you here?' She frowned her amazement. 'Here? At the library?'

'Please.'

'But surely it is your place to visit him?'

'That is true. You are perfectly correct. I should and I would if it were possible.' Curt shifted uncomfortably, looking abashed. 'Unfortunately it isn't.'

'May I ask why?'

Because death could be waiting at every crossing, every junction, every roof he would have to pass. But he could never explain that. Not to her.

'May I rely on your discretion?' He didn't wait for an answer. 'I suffer from agoraphobia. You must have heard of it. A fear of open spaces. That is why I asked if I could stay here for six hours. I had arranged to be collected by a friend. That isn't possible, now, I know, but I really must get in touch with the doctor. I have information he will appreciate and time is of the essence. I promise he will thank you if you make the effort and I most certainly will be grateful.'

He was tall, well-dressed, handsome and, most important, polite.

'Well,' she said reluctantly. 'I'll try.'

'Thank you. Please. One other thing. Tell him you have found an accident prone. In reverse!'

6

Doctor Fenshaw arrived an hour later. A large man, no longer young, one wearing a shabby suit and a frayed shirt. He came when Curt had almost given up hope. He entered the cubicle his bulk almost filling the available space. Curt rose, offering him the use of the single chair, and leaned against the wall after he had drawn the curtain.

'Thank you for coming.'

Fenshaw grunted, eased his bulk into a more comfortable position. 'So you're the mystery man. Name?' He nodded as Curt gave it. 'You've made quite an impression on Lucy. I hope you haven't made a fool of her and wasted my time.'

'I haven't.'

'Glad to hear it. Why did you insist that I come here?'

'I'm afraid,' said Curt simply. 'You may think I'm crazy, doctor, and then again you may not. It's a chance I have to take.'

'Suppose you let me be the judge of that?' Fenshaw wheezed as he fumbled in his brief case and produced a thick pad of ruled paper. Curt guessed he had also activated a recording device but made no comment. 'Now, Lucy said you had something important to tell me. She mentioned an accident prone. One in reverse. That's a peculiar statement to make. So peculiar that I've gone to quite a bit of trouble getting down here. I hope my journey has not been wasted.'

'It hasn't.' Curt glanced at his wristwatch. Time was passing faster than he liked. 'Would you be interested to learn that my death has been predicted by a cybernetic machine to take place within the next three hours? Accurately predicted, I mean, with a probability factor of 99.99 per cent.'

'The Oracle?'

'Yes. I'm surprised you know about it.'

'It's a badly kept secret. Or perhaps a secret that isn't supposed to be too well guarded. Leaks arouse curiosity and stimulate interest. If what I've heard is true then, once certain details have been clarified, access will be offered to selected clients and, in time, the public. Booths,' he explained. 'Like the old telephone ones. Go in, pay your fee, don a helmet and ask your question. Once on the market those behind it will make a fortune. They should. They claim the answers are never wrong.'

'That's what has me worried. I came here because I thought a library would be a safe haven. While waiting I read your book. It struck me that you would probably be able to help me. Will you?'

'Help you?' Fenshaw looked puzzled. 'How?'

'You know all about accident prones. Those around whom accidents continually happen. Three times now, within a few hours, I've had narrow escapes from death. I was almost crushed beneath the falling body of a suicide. I almost fell down the shaft of an elevator. The third time a wheel fell off a stratoliner and crushed the car I had just left. Three accidents, each of them potentially fatal, each caused by a wildly improbable combination of time, place and circumstance. Would you say that such coincidences were normal?'

'Unusual, perhaps, but it could happen and, if what you say is true, it did.'

'It's true, right enough, and that isn't all.' Rapidly Curt told the doctor about the thirty-six men who had returned from Venus and died by suicide or freak accident. He mentioned Medway and touched again on the supposedly infallible machine which had predicted his death. When he finished a thin film of sweat dewed his features and his hands trembled a little. 'So you see, Fenshaw, I'm in trouble. If the Oracle can be trusted then I'm due to die within three hours.' He checked his watch. 'Less than three.'

'Not necessarily,' said Fenshaw. 'The prediction for your death within six hours was exactly the same for both nine and twelve hours. It is quite possible that, even though you had a high probability factor for the six-hour period, you will be safe for the whole twelve hours.'

'No. The Oracle can't give a hundred per cent probability. It has to take into account the unknown factor which could, as was explained to me, just possibly invalidate its prediction.' Curt added, grimly, 'As I see it that's my only hope. The unknown factor — God knows what it could be!'

'Maybe there's more to it than that,' said Fenshaw thoughtfully. 'If it was so probable that you would die within the six hour period then why bother with the nine and twelve hour ones? If the first was right the others would be unnecessary. However, let's not waste time speculating on the logic of a construct.' He riffled his papers. 'Your story interests me. I have examined several hundred accident prones but never have I found one who claimed to operate in reverse.'

'You would hardly expect to,' said Curt dryly. 'They would have died before they could even guess anything was wrong.'

'Admitted, but it is a new field of research. I am deeply interested in it. Deeply interested.' Fenshaw stared at the blank screen of the computer. 'First some questions then, with your permission, I'd like to run some tests on you. I have the equipment in my private laboratory back home.'

'Is it far?'

172

'About fifteen minutes.'

Curt shook his head. 'Later, maybe, I'd rather not leave here just yet. But I'm willing to answer your questions.'

'Good.' Fenshaw adjusted his pad of ruled paper. 'Have you ever experienced any other accidents prior to your journey to Venus?'

'A few, no more than seemed normal. Some broken crockery. A slip down some stairs. A twisted ankle. The usual trifling things that annoy rather than concern.'

'I see. And while you were on Venus?'

'At the Station? None.'

'How do you mean 'none?' Did any accidents of any kind take place while you were there?'

'I . . . ' Curt frowned, thinking. 'Now that you make a point of it there weren't. Not one. Not even a cut finger or an unexpected fall. I was there six months and I never saw or heard of an accident.'

'I see. And after your return?'

'There was the stratoliner breakdown. It made me late for my appointment, but it was a normal thing, one of the engines cut out.'

'Normal?' Fenshaw raised his eyebrows. 'With the maintenance those engines have?' He made a note on his pad. 'Anything else?'

'Nothing until I arrived to keep my appointment. I'd been working on some Martian artifacts and had gone to England on vacation. Everything seemed normal until I got here. Then Benwick almost killed me when he jumped from the roof.'

'As you said. Then the machine predicted your death and you almost fell down the elevator shaft.'

'No. The accident with the elevator came before the machine made its prediction.'

Fenshaw made another note then nodded and eased his bulk in the chair.

'So it boils down to this. We can discount the engine failure, it was hardly an accident and it didn't threaten you personally. The suicide just missed you, but he also just missed others and you weren't the only one in danger of being crushed. Again I'd discount that as a personal accident. The elevator shaft is in a different category. Tell me, did the other men with you hang back at all?'

'Medway and the Director?'

'Yes.'

'How do you mean?'

'Did they wait for you to get in front of them? It would be natural for a younger man to be impatient. You could have been manipulated to enter the elevator first.'

'I don't remember,' said Curt.' Is it important?'

'It could be. Of all the accidents you've told me about that with the elevator shaft is the most suspect.'

'I don't understand what you're getting at.'

'No? Look at it this way,' urged Fenshaw. 'Suppose that it wasn't an accident at all. That the misleading signals and the failure of the cage to stop as it should have had been arranged? What would you call it then?'

The answer was obvious. 'An attempt at murder.'

7

It was a tempting thought. Human enemies were understandable, the danger from them could be guarded against, but . . .

Curt shook his head.

'You don't agree?' Fenshaw shrugged. 'As you wish. Now, to continue, when you left the building you took a cab to the airport and barely escaped with your life when a wheel, falling from a stratoliner in flight, crushed it. Another unusual occurrence, true, but that could be all. So, to sum up, you've had a couple of near misses. That isn't anything abnormal. Sometimes these things run in sequence. You know the old saying about 'things coming in three's.' I think it possible that you are worrying without cause.'

'Is that really what you believe?'

'Yes. I do.'

'Then what about the other men? Why should they all have died?

'I'm not interested in the other men. It doesn't matter about them. They can't all be as you claim to be, accident prones in reverse. Meaning you all attract lethal danger to yourselves. But only recently, or you would have all died years ago. If there is any connection there has to be a common factor. Something you all did or shared or . . . ' Fenshaw broke off, then slammed his hand down hard against his pad. 'Fool! It's been dangling before me all the time. You have all been to Venus.'

'Not at the same time.'

'That needn't be important. There seems to be a delay factor in the return and the demise. You were the latest and the last. Correct?'

'That's right.'

'So there seems to be a pattern. Something drove those others to kill themselves. What?'

'If I knew that I would know everything.' Curt shifted his weight against the wall. 'That is the answer Carter is looking for. The one he needs to find. Until he does he dare not recall any more men from Venus. Not when every returned worker dies within a year after reaching Earth. Already there has to be someone, somewhere, curious about the deaths. Some newscaster or a relative or even someone like yourself making a study of the effects of spaceflight. Once the truth gets out the IDC is in deep trouble. Even if they rescue and compensate the workers they will never be able to replace them.'

'An obvious conclusion,' said Fenshaw dryly. 'Let's take it further. What common factor, aside from having been to Venus, unites you and those others? What experience did you share? You are one of them. What happened to them must have happened to you. What was it?'

'Spaceflight?' Curt saw the doctor's expression of annoyance. 'What else? But that can't be the answer because those returning from Mars and Luna are not affected.'

'Then it must be something peculiar to Venus. Think, man! What common thing did you all do on arrival? On departure? While working?'

'We breathed the same air, ate the same

food, wore the same clothing. We all lived the same way because we had no choice. The Station is a box. One set in a furnace. Have you any idea of what Venus is really like?'

'Tell me.'

'Later, maybe, now I haven't the time. And it isn't important. I'm alive and I intend to remain that way. If I had something in common with the rest wouldn't I be dead by now?'

'Isn't that what you're afraid of? Dying? If you're not then why am I here?'

'Of course I'm afraid of dying. Who isn't? Do you think I enjoy knowing that some damned machine has given me only a few hours to live? Normal death is bad enough but to know you are going to die within a certain time, that nothing you can do will stop it! Damn it, Fenshaw! That's execution!'

'Relax. Panic won't help.'

'What will?' Curt glanced at his watch. 'Don't play with me. Time is running out. I've less than two hours. If you can help me at all get on with it.'

'I can't do anything here. You'll have to

come to my laboratory. I have instruments there capable of measuring the electronic potential of the cortex. I must determine if your ESP factor has diverged from the norm.'

'What has that to do with it?'

'Maybe everything.' Fenshaw rose from his chair. 'The paraphysical sciences are still relatively new and we have only scratched the surface of the hidden potential of the human mind. Telepathy. Teleportation. Telekinesis, we are stumbling on the verge of finding out just how and why they work. In my investigation of accident prones I discovered that they have a different extra sensory perception factor to normal people. It is almost as if they are human accumulators of a strange type of energy which in some way affects the Heisenburg Uncertainty Principle.'

'Go on.'

'Let me put it this way. It is theoretically possible for anything to happen. Literally, that is. The Moon could fall to the Earth. The Sun could go out. The Universe could collapse. These things don't happen because the probability against them doing so is so high that for all practical purposes they don't exist. An accident prone alters that.'

'How?'

'The probability of a wheel falling off a stratoliner in flight and crushing a cab is so remote as to be in the realm of utter impossibility. However an accident prone seems to have the ability to alter the Heisenburg Principle. Things which are impossible become merely improbable. Things which are highly improbable become less so. And so we get a succession of inexplicable accidents.'

'Are you saying that all the men who returned from Venus are accident prones?'

'Perhaps, but as you said accident prones in reverse. However it isn't as simple as that. The great majority of the men committed suicide. I'd like to know just why.'

'I don't feel any desire to kill myself,' said Curt. 'If it applied to the others then why not to me?'

'That,' said Fenshaw grimly, 'is what we're going to find out.'

He led the way from the cubicle, pausing at the desk to say something to the woman who nodded and looked sorrowfully at Curt as he followed the doctor through the doors.

'I told her you were a little confused about things,' he said. 'Lucy is a good woman but tends to talk a little. It would be better if she forgot the stranger suffering from agoraphobia with an interest in odd subjects. Suit you?'

'Yes.'

'Good, we'll get a ride.' Fenshaw stared down the road looking for a passing cab.

Curt accompanied him, not greatly caring what they did or where they went. For some reason his mind seemed dull, his spirits low. He was no longer concerned about the predictions of the Oracle and a thick, vitality-sapping depression closed around him.

He didn't even realize that he was walking.

Memories woke, taking dominance in his mind. Venus, the Station in which he had spent a long six months, fighting heat, fear, monotony, boredom. A specialist, using his talents to smooth the path of existence, to recognize a host of potential dangers and prevent them before they could happen. A precaution Carter had taken knowing what could happen when too many men were squeezed into an area too small in conditions no sane man could accept. To the Interplanetary Development Corporation he had been a wise investment. One who had more than earned his high reward. There had been no trouble. Now, it seemed, he had become surplus to requirements.

Something tore at his arm. Something else shrilled with a thin, high-pitched screaming and a blow on his thigh numbed his leg.

'What . . . ?'

Fenshaw had him by the shoulder, his face tense, his eyes glaring. Just past him a car had come to a halt. It had slewed against the kerb and mounted the sidewalk. The driver looked about to vomit.

'You damned fool!' Fenshaw yielded to anger and shook Curt like a dog. 'If I hadn't manage to grab you and pull you back you'd be dead! What's the matter with you? Do you want to die?'

'No.' Curt shook his head, trying to clear his senses. 'What happened?'

'You stepped into the road as if you were asleep. If I hadn't been quick that car would have hit you. You'd be broken, crushed, dead. You wouldn't have stood a chance.' He added, caustically, 'A hell of a way to solve your problem.'

8

It had been a moment of forgetfulness, an instant of carelessness, but it had almost cost him his life. Lanson had died like that. He had stepped in front of a car and had paid for his stupidity. Now he had done the same. If it hadn't been for the doctor he, too, would be nothing but skin and broken bone, pulped flesh and scattered blood.

What had made him do it?

His thigh hurt and he rubbed the bruised flesh. He couldn't win. So far he had been lucky. Twice since the Oracle had predicted his death he had been saved by apparent miracles. But how long would they last? And even if he did manage to live through the first six-hour period what of the next? The third? He realized that his own mental narrowing of the time limit could lead to his own danger.

He had started off by being super-cautious.

A shadow had made him run for his life and his instinctive reaction had carried him clear of the falling wheel. But that caution hadn't lasted. He had relaxed, daydreamed, lost full awareness of the external world — and had tried to walk into the path of a speeding vehicle.

Next time there would be no friendly hand to save him. A warning shadow to make him run. Next time it would be death just as it had for the others. Had they, too, dreamed of Venus before meeting their end?

Fenshaw said, 'If we're going to get anywhere we'd best get moving. The sooner I do the tests the better.' He frowned at Curt's expression. 'You do want to have the tests?'

'No. I don't think so. Later, maybe, but not now.'

'Why not?'

'I don't feel right. Something odd is happening. I seem to be slipping in some way. Back then, when you saved me, I was thinking about Venus. Nothing else was in my mind. Just memories of the Station and the conditions we had to suffer and the fear we had to conquer. It blotted everything else out. I don't remember the road, the car, anything. That's why I almost died. Would have died if you hadn't saved me. Was that why I sent for you? Had I a conviction I would need you? I don't know. But I don't think I can beat the Oracle. I don't think I can beat anything any more.'

He fought for breath feeling a sudden tightening of his chest, a frightening tension of his nerves. Why continue the struggle? Why not end it all now? One step, one small step into the path of an approaching car and it would be over. It would be so easy. One step. Just one step. One step . . .

He gasped as Fenshaw's palm cracked against his cheek.

'Harris! What's the matter with you? Snap out of it!'

'Sorry.' Curt hardly felt the pain of the slap. 'I was drifting again.'

Back to Venus. Back to the Station listening to the noises all around, the moans and curses and, too often, the sobs of those deep in self-pity. Watching the tribulations of those with too much imagination. Others who prayed for death. Those who fought to be detached. Seeing the concept of sanity slowly alter. If, to be sane, meant to live in Hell, then to be mad was to escape. But to be mad in such an environment was to invite destruction. Drugs helped as did femmikins, books, tapes, games, hypnosis, comfort, companionship, manipulation. The continual assurance that it was all going to end. That soon they would be back home where they could roll in snow and stand in chilling rain and sleep on ice if they wished. Golden promises to help them combat the endless heat. To cool their minds if nothing else. To help them sleep and dream of endless vistas of arctic chill.

'You drifting again?' Fenshaw was losing patience. 'Or are you thinking of killing yourself? Is that your solution to your problem.'

Curt stared at him with stunned realization. 'Man, you're a genius!'

'What?'

'That's the solution. What you just

said.' He gave the doctor no time to comment. 'I told you I was drifting. Going back, in memory, to my time at the Station. I was in a bind and my subconscious was trying to tell me something. Something else was trying to block it so I couldn't get it clear. Then you gave me the answer. The solution.'

'To kill yourself?'

'Just that. Is there a Hibernation Centre in the city?'

'We've got three.'

'Take me to the nearest. Hurry, doctor. Please! I've no time to waste!'

In the cab Fenshaw said. 'What's on your mind?'

'Don't you get it? The Oracle predicted that I will die within six hours. I'm convinced now that prediction is true. I will die, nothing can stop that, so what's the point of fighting against it? But I can choose the way I shall go.'

'Are you insane?'

'Far from it.' Curt glanced at his watch and tensed at what he saw. 'You know what happens at a Hibernation Centre?'

'Naturally.'

'Well, then. Isn't it technically true that a person in deep freeze dies?'

'Technically, perhaps,' admitted Fenshaw slowly. 'The heart stops beating. There is no circulation. The tissues and blood freeze. There is no respiration. Yes, I think it safe to say that, in the accepted sense of the word, the clients of a Hibernation Centre are dead.'

'Exactly!' Curt stared triumphantly at his companion. 'The Oracle has predicted I will die. So, with a little help, I will do just that and whatever is hounding me will be satisfied. The fact I can be revived after the danger period has nothing to do with it.'

'You think that it will work?' Fenshaw wasn't as confident. 'You hope to cheat fate but what if fate refuses to be cheated? Not everyone can be revived. Quite a few clients die. How can you be sure you won't be one of them?'

'I can't. But I have to take the chance.'

Hibernation was a fad and in earlier times would have been forbidden but, in the swelling growth of the right of individual freedom, people had won their liberation from the smothering dictates of politicians obsessed with control.

It had its uses. The elderly extended their remaining years in the hope that new discoveries in the future would restore their youth and beauty. Others used it as a form of vacation. Some for easing a broken romance. Others to gain forgetfulness together with the bored, the disenchanted, the lonely, the ill.

Suspended animation. Available to all — if they could pay the high fees.

It had its dangers. Not everyone was successfully revived. Sometimes they couldn't withstand the impact of powerful drugs, the shock of freezing and later thawing, the halting of all the normal processes of living. Most came through but it was made clear that responsibility rested with the individual. That those who chose to gamble had to bear the loss.

Curt had nothing to lose. At the reception desk he was too conscious of the passing of time to waste any in the usual interchange. No delicate counselling, no warnings of what might be, no subtle testing as to his genuine standing as a potential client.

Displaying his credit card he said, 'Use this and book me in for a day.'

'What?' The receptionist was startled. 'You must be joking, sir. No one wants to hibernate for only a day. In any case it can't be done. It simply isn't possible.'

'How long, then?'

'At least a week. Then the revivification will take at least a couple of days. It cannot be accelerated, the danger is too great.'

'Damn it all, man, don't argue with me!' Curt bit his lip as he checked his watch. If he was to die now — when he was so close . . . 'Use that card and book me in,' he snapped. 'I must be deep frozen within forty minutes. Revive me in the shortest possible time. Hurry!'

Later, as he rested naked in the vat, waiting for the onset of deep freeze, he had time to think and worry. Drugs flowed in his veins, guarding him against pain, robbing him of fear, easing his tormented spirit and bestowing a warm euphoria, but his mind was still active.

Would his plan work? Would his action

fulfil the cybernetic prediction? Would the Oracle, if consulted, report him dead? Would he rise from his frigid bed? Or would fate laugh at his efforts and end the conflict by bringing real death?

He didn't know. He couldn't know. And, as he watched the swinging hands of a large clock against the wall swing towards zero hour, he just didn't care.

He was going to die. In that the Oracle had been correct but the main problem still remained.

Why should he die at all? What was the thing that hounded all those who had returned from Venus?

Then the sharp, touch of chill over as soon as it had registered.

Softly the chronometer marked the zero hour, the end of the six-hour prediction and, in the vat, Curt's dead body rested in a film of ice.

9

A wakening and the slow return of awareness. Discomfort merging with the brittle scintillation of light, the droning impact of sound, the stir and flow of returning life. Curt moved his arms, his legs, his fingers. He opened his eyes, squinting against the glare, then, with feeble slowness, sat upright and looked around.

He was in a room all of green. The walls were a soft pastel, the ceiling a lighter shade, the floor a deep emerald. Machines lined the walls together with racks of medicines and drugs, hypoguns for their administration and other objects he could not identify.

'How do you feel?'

Curt stared at the other occupant of the room. He, too, was dressed all in green; the colour of grass and vegetation, of spring and hope and life. A young and enthusiastic man beneath his smock and cap and gloves. A medical attendant enjoying another successful resurrection.

He smiled and Curt smiled back.

'I'm feeling fine.' The truth, the pain had vanished. 'At least I'm alive. How long?'

'Twelve days.'

'What? I ordered the minimum.'

'And you got it. We couldn't attempt to revive you until the process had finished its cycle. If we had tried we could have lost. Anyway, what difference does a few days make?'

'None, I guess. The main thing is that I'm alive.' Curt stretched, feeling the tension, enjoying the relaxation of his muscles. 'How soon can I leave?'

'About an hour. Give the eddy currents a chance to equalize your temperature.'

'Right. Any chance of coffee?'

'Sorry, no.' The attendant added, 'There is someone waiting for you. A doctor, he said. He's been hanging around for two days now.'

'Fenshaw,' said Curt. 'You can let him know I'm fine and will be with him as soon as you let me out of this place.'

Alone he yielded to a sudden fatigue and lying back on the pneumatic mattress closed his eyes.

He was alive!

The predicted period had passed and he was still alive. He had beaten the Oracle. Won the gamble. Made a mock of the prediction — or had he?

He felt his mind begin to churn as he tried to resolve the paradox. The machine had predicted that he would die. He had accepted temporary death to escape the prediction of the machine. And yet, by doing so, he had made the prediction come true.

Which came first, the chicken or the egg?

Two hours later he smiled at Fenshaw as the doctor rose from his chair. He looked haggard, tired, his age accentuated by the lines marring his features. A man genuinely concerned who visibly relaxed as he recognized his vigil was over.

'Curt! How do you feel?'

'Fine. Better than you by the look of it. Quite well, really, for a man who is supposed to be dead.'

'Still worried about that?' Fenshaw led the way to the exit. 'Well, it's natural, I suppose. I want to get you to my laboratory and run some tests. Are you ready?'

'Slow down, doctor. You forget that I haven't eaten for days. I'm hungry. Let's find a restaurant.'

'I've been working on your problem,' Fenshaw said, sipping coffee as Curt ate a large meal. 'I tried to interview Carter but you don't just walk in on the Director of IDC. Even so I did manage to gain access to the records. Some friends,' he explained. 'Mutual contacts. As you suspected there does seem to be a definite trace of some influence against those who died. The incidence of suicide is abnormal and the accidents grotesque.'

'As I told you. When you tried to contact the Director did you tell them about me?'

'Of course not. You weren't mentioned. I didn't think it wise. To them I was just another crazed academic hunting material for another book.'

'Did you discover what caused the deaths?'

'No.' Fenshaw sipped at his coffee. 'The common factor is still missing. Obviously it has to be something uniting you all but, as you are the only one left alive and as you don't seem to know what it is then it's pretty hopeless to find out. That part of the programme doesn't interest me. Your theory of 'reverse accident prones' does. I really believe you are on the right trail there.'

The doctor signalled for more coffee.

'Look at it this way,' he suggested after the waitress had refilled his cup. 'We know an accident prone has an ESP factor different to the norm. We also know that the planets are surrounded by layers of energy, that on Earth was once called the Heaviside Layer. Does it strike you as possible that a living person, subjected to the differing impact of such layers, might somehow be affected by them?'

'Sorry, doctor, your theory doesn't hold water. What about those manning the orbiting stations? They don't seem to be affected. Neither do those from the moon and Mars. Anyway, conditions on Venus are unique.'

'So I've discovered,' said Fenshaw. 'I've done my research. The planet is a literal furnace. What made the IDC go to such trouble and expense?'

'Money,' said Curt. 'Power. Ambition.'

'But . . . '

'Add greed to that. The thrill of exploration. Of building something new. Of rebellion. All because of what was found on Venus. The tri-polar crystals have made the IDC what it is today.'

'I still find it hard to understand. Way back an initial probe condemned the entire planet.'

'True, but as Carter pointed out what if an alien race had sent a probe to Earth? One that had landed in the Antarctic? What kind of message would it have sent back? How would heat-loving creatures have reacted? So he authorized other probes and an orbiting vessel to monitor them. Venus is a furnace, right enough, but there are varying areas of heat-intensity. One was found of relative coolness. A tremendous caldera. A probe checked it and scooped out a load of shale. Among it the tri-polar crystals were found.'

199

'History,' said Fenshaw, 'but it doesn't help us. Let's concentrate on the men. They died as you almost died, by sheer, unthinking carelessness. What could have caused that?'

Curt shrugged, pushing aside his empty plate.

'Depression? A psychologist told me once that every man secretly yearns to die. Sometimes, when the death-wish gets too strong, he will do stupid things like stepping into a busy road, balancing on the edge of a high roof, taking a chance on whether or not a cartridge will fire if he pulls the trigger. Could that be it?'

'Do you desire to die?'

'No longer. I've been there, done that and . . . ' Curt broke off, no longer jocular as Fenshaw grabbed at his chest. 'Something wrong?'

'Just a twinge. Indigestion, maybe, or . . . ' He winced at another attack then relaxed a little. 'All right, it's going now. Don't worry about it. I'm fine.'

'You don't look it.' Curt looked for the waitress then, remembering, dug his hand into his pockets searching for the packet

Carter had given him. The one containing medication that had helped him and could help the doctor. 'Here!' He found what he had looked for and spilled a tablet from the crumpled foil. 'Take this. Get it down. Hurry!'

'What is it?'

'Chemical magic. Something to steady the heart, lungs, nerves and all the rest of it. I got them from the Director and Carter would only have the best. 'Move! Chew and swallow. It will help.' He set his coffee before the doctor. 'Take a drink! Do it!'

He checked the packet as the doctor obeyed. The foil was thick, reluctant to yield, when it did he held it over his palm, shaking it to clear it of its contents. Four tablets fell into his palm — and something else.

'What?' Curt stared at it with shocked disbelief. 'How did that get in there?'

'What is it?' Fenshaw, his discomfort eased by the medication, leaned forward, squinting as he stared at what lay in his companion's palm. 'It looks like an ornament. A large bead.'

'It isn't a bead.' Curt rolled it from his hand to lie on the table as he replaced the tablets within the foil. 'That is a Venusian tri-polar crystal — and I've never owned one in my life!'

10

It lay before them, a thing no larger than a small olive, oddly modulated and with a strange and compelling beauty. Light shimmered over it, a scintillate, ever-changing medley of hues. Something which had once held the savage glow of furnace-heat now looking like a fire opal with the sheen of a pearl.

It was beautiful and yet, somehow, there was menace as well. It seemed to glow like the feral eye of some alien beast and the pulsating shimmer had a strange, almost hypnotic fascination.

'It's beautiful.' Fenshaw leaned even closer to the shining object. 'A Venusian crystal, you say?'

'That's what it is. They are used in the vast majority of industrial computers. They are capable of holding a tremendous amount of information. Basically they are a million tiny crystals bonded into one. In effect they are to a microchip as the chip is to the transistors that replaced the old vacuum tubes. The heart of our technological progress.'

'So they are valuable.' The doctor touched it with the tip of his finger. 'And rare.'

'Valuable, yes, rare too. But not on Venus. All you need to do there is to scoop them up. The hard part is doing it.'

A comment which brought back the past. The adventure that had trembled too close to nightmare when he had joined the others in the Station.

'It took a dozen years to get established,' he explained when Fenshaw asked. 'First the IDC had to determine the value of the crystals. Then they got to work. In reality the conglomerates own and run the world. Earth is their domain, the politicians nothing but their strutting lackeys. Money is power and they know how to use it. Soon they will gain an empire. The one in space. Mars, Venus the moon and, in time, Jupiter and its satellites. The entire solar system. The IDC will control it all.'

'You don't like them.'

'Why do you say that?'

'The way you're talking. It gives that impression.'

'I'm talking recent history.' Curt touched the shimmering crystal. 'That's what this is all about. Look on the bright side. Expansion usually is accompanied by liberation. Old regulations are discarded, old rules tossed aside, petty restrictions made by petty politicians dumped where they belong. When the IDC established the lunar domes they didn't ask for permission. They just made a place in which people could live and work. No concern about pollution, waste disposal and all the rest of it. No fretting about the environment. Just build and mine and convert and simply dump all the rubbish into the nearest crater. If nothing else they got the job done. And they did it fast.'

'As they did on Mars.'

'That's right. Everyone knew the moon had no air or water but they were wrong. The moon has plenty of both locked into the rocks. Together with metals and chemicals and all the rest of it. What's so strange about that? The moon is a miniature world and, maybe a long time ago, it was like Earth. The same with Mars.'

'And now it's the turn of Venus.' Fenshaw shook his head. 'The things you get into when you don't expect it. I take a tablet and get a lecture.'

'Sorry.'

'Don't apologize. I found it interesting.'

'You're sure you feel better now?'

'I'm fine.' Fenshaw added, slowly, 'One thing — why did you go to Venus?'

'For the money.'

'I'm serious.'

'So am I. What, in our society, is worth more? With money you can buy anything you want.' Curt paused. 'There was more,' he admitted. 'The challenge. The novelty of doing something only a few had as yet done. To find how good I was when it came to the crunch. But you don't want to hear about that.'

'Wrong. We've a problem to solve, remember? The more data I can gather the better. Who knows what scrap of information might help? So — ?'

'They needed the Station because they couldn't gather the crystals fast enough. There had to be a continuous supply. The Station makes that possible. They constructed most of it on the moon — low gravity made it easier to ship it out. All prefabricated, formed into bundles, thrown into space to head for an orbit around Venus. Waiting vessels collected them, manoeuvred them into an assembly area, then lowered them into the caldera. More work and building going on until the construction was finished enough to get into production. That would be about a year ago.' He added, 'If you want some idea of the scope of the enterprise it matches that of the ancient Egyptian building of the pyramids.'

'And we still don't know how they did it,' said Fenshaw. 'So it commenced operation six months before you joined them?'

'That's right.'

'And?'

'Things were going wrong. Fights, quarrels, lowered production. We called it that though we didn't really produce anything. Just collected the crystals. Carter selected me to sort things out. I did. As best as I could.'

'Want to tell me?'

'The Station is a box as I told you. A prison if you like. All you can do is work, sweat, eat a little, sleep a little, work some more. The way we collect the crystals is by using clone-adjuncts. You lift a hand it lifts a hand, you walk it walks, and so on. The klants, that's what we call them, are metal skeletons electronically connected to a full body-form and headset. The headset relays what's outside. Filters cut the glare.'

'Remote control machines. They stay outside?'

'Until they are due for maintenance. Then they come in and cool down. It takes time.'

'I can imagine,' said Fenshaw. 'How did they collect the crystals?'

'They didn't. The men controlling them did. They had to dig into the shale and sieve what they found and sort it as best they could. Sometimes they would slip and you'd hear them screaming. They weren't hurt, of course, not physically, but mentally they had fallen into a searing inferno.' Curt paused, remembering, then shook his head. The incident was long over, the memories faded but, too often, he woke sweating with terror. 'That's enough history.'

'But you solved the problem?'

'The best I could,' said Curt. 'I changed the shifts, the duties, the games. I made up a competition and taught them how to relax.'

'With the femmikins?'

'They helped.'

'They would. Women are beginning to hate them. Too many men prefer them to the real thing. But you couldn't have a mixed-sex crew on a place like the Station.' Fenshaw looked at the crystal, drinking in its beauty. 'Would you mind if I borrowed this? There are some tests I'd like to make. On you too, if you're ready.'

'Take the crystal, and keep it,' said Curt. 'I don't like the things. But leave me out. I don't want to take your tests.'

'They can't hurt you.'

'Maybe, but I've the same feeling I had when Carter tried to get me to don the helmet of the Oracle. Call it a hunch, if you like, but I don't want to be examined.'

'As you please.' Fenshaw wasn't annoyed. 'My investigations into the paraphysical sciences have taught me that so-called 'hunches' are something more than an old wives' tale. Unless a subject is willing to cooperate, his very reluctance will create conditions in which only negative results are possible.'

He took a sip of the coffee, now cold.

'That is why dice players always try to convince themselves that the dice they throw will produce the number they want. They don't know why they do it, of course, but I have proved that a positive condition is able to affect the paraphysical result. In other words, if a dice player believes hard enough that he will throw a seven, then he will throw it. The ancients called it 'faith' and they were quite correct when they stated it was the strongest force known to man.'

'So I haven't any faith?'

'Have you, Curt? I doubt it.' Fenshaw pushed aside the coffee cup in what Curt recognized as a symbolical gesture. 'The way you are feeling now tells me that you don't really expect me to discover anything that will help you. While you feel that way you are right. I cannot fight against your convictions. The way we are now I am simply wasting my time. A pity. I would have liked to find the answer.'

Rising he held out his hand.

'If you should change your mind contact me. Contact me anyway, I'd like to keep in touch.'

Curt nodded, touched the proffered hand and remained at the table, staring through the window as the doctor paid the bill and left the restaurant. For a moment he hesitated on the sidewalk as if undecided what to do then, with sudden determination, he stepped forward and hailed a cab.

The vehicle slowed and swept towards the edge of the road to halt before the doctor. Curt saw him bend, obviously to give the driver his destination, and watched, not really interested, as he opened the rear door and began to enter the passenger compartment.

Something like a pistol shot echoed down the street.

A yellow car jerked towards the kerb, rubber hanging in tattered ribbons from its front wheel. It slewed, seemed about to topple then, with a screaming of metal on metal, plunged directly into the rear of the halted cab.

11

The ambulance had come and gone. The police had taken details and left. The crumpled ruin of the two vehicles had been towed away and the street was as it had been before the incident had occurred. Only then did Curt leave the restaurant.

He strode cautiously along the street, suspicious, too aware that, still, he walked in danger. The doctor's demise had proved that and he headed a list of questions that Curt had been trying to resolve.

Fenshaw was dead — fact number one.

He had been less than happy — fact number two.

He had carried a Venusian crystal — fact number three.

Where had it come from?

He didn't like the Venusian gems and his experiences in the Station had hardened his distaste. He had been glad

213

to get rid of it, but how had it come into his possession?

The crystals were still rare enough to have maintained their value and no one would casually dispose of one without good reason. Who would have access to them? When and how had the thing been planted on him? Why?

Would Fenshaw have died if he had not possessed the crystal?

Curt frowned with sudden suspicion and halted, oblivious to the stares of other pedestrians. The thing he and Fenshaw had been searching for. The common link connecting the Venus-returns. He hadn't shared that link, not voluntarily, but he'd been given no choice.

He signalled a cab. 'Interplanet Building. Hurry!'

The receptionist stared at him as he strode towards the desk, her eyes wide with shocked incredulity.

'Carter,' he snapped. 'I must see him!'

'Mr. Harris! I thought . . . '

'Never mind what you thought!' Impatience made his tone savage. 'Just tell the Director I'm here and that it's important I see him.'

'Yes, sir, but he isn't available at the moment.' Her fingers danced over the keyboard of her computer. 'He's at a meeting but . . . '

'Just tell him I'm here. While waiting I'll see your Chief of Security.'

Access was immediate. Curt came straight to the point.

'There was an accident a short while ago. Two men were involved, the driver of the cab and his passenger. The driver was injured. The dead man was Doctor Fenshaw. It is important that you collect his clothing and personal effects. Waste no time. Understood?'

'The location?'

'Sorry.' Curt gave it. 'This is IDC business. Report to the Director when it's done.'

Fifteen minutes later he was ushered into a familiar office.

Carter stared at him as if seeing a ghost.

'Harris! But you are dead!'

'For a dead man I'm pretty active, don't you think? But you have it wrong.

The Oracle predicted I would die, yes, and I did die. Luckily nothing was said about the death having to be permanent. I hibernated for twelve days and here I am.'

'Incredible! Medway, did you hear that?'

'I heard it.' The thin man hunched a little deeper in his chair. 'No wonder you seemed to have vanished. Are you ready to be examined now?'

'No.'

'Why not?'

'Fenshaw asked me the same question. He's dead now. Killed in an accident meant for me. But you must know all about that.' To Carter he said, 'He was carrying a tri-polar crystal. I've ordered security to collect his things. It will be among them.'

'Does the Chief know what he is looking for?' He smiled as Curt shook his head. 'You're discrete. I like that. The Chief is also discrete but it will help if he has more information.' He busied himself with the intercom then returned his attention to Curt. 'He'll find it. If it's

216

been stolen he'll track it down. I know it has monetary value but, aside from that, why do you think it so important?'

'It holds the answer.'

'To what?' Carter gestured towards a chair. 'Sit down, Harris. Relax. You want something to drink? Eat?'

'No thank you. I'm not hungry or thirsty and I'm not deranged or deluded. When I say the crystals have the answer I mean it.'

Medway said, 'Then you must be examined. Your knowledge incorporated in the cybernetic machine.'

'No.'

'Why not?' This time it was the Director who fired the question. 'You know our situation. We have two hundred men ready for recall. Are you going to return them to their deaths?'

'No.' Curt leaned back and stared thoughtfully at the Director and Medway. 'I have solved the problem. I know what caused the deaths of those thirty-six men. I know what almost caused my own death. I know what killed Fenshaw. When I said the crystals had the answer I should have said they *are* the answer. They are the common factor.'

Medway was scornful. 'Are you serious? A crystal is nothing but a lump of inanimate matter. How could it kill anyone?'

Carter ignored the comment. He said, 'If you've solved the problem, Harris, then tell us what to do about it.'

'That is simple. Just make certain that none of the returnees brings back a crystal with them.'

'They don't. They can't. The crystals are the property of the Interplanetary Development Corporation. Contraband.'

'Sure,' said Curt dryly. 'And every worker is a good, clean, loyal and honest servant of the IDC. Humble serfs who will obey any order without question. Maybe a few of them are but you won't find them on the Station. There you'll find them on the brink of rebellion, half-crazed, wanting to hurt, to destroy, to ease their pain in any way they can. The tri-polar crystals are valuable. Robbing the IDC of one would be a small victory and everyone wants to win.'

'So they steal.'

'Why not? They have worked for those crystals, sweated for them, risked their lives and sanity to get them. They figure they have a right to them. A token of victory.'

'Did you get yours?'

'Not on the Station. I didn't try and the others didn't offer to help. I was an outsider,' Curt explained. 'A company man sent to snoop around and, maybe, see what others thought I shouldn't. But I learned. Just make sure no one smuggles a crystal back to Earth as a souvenir or memento.'

'That should be easy.' Medway was sarcastic. 'Strip and body searches. Confiscation of clothes and personal effects. Scanning. Enemas . . . ' He shrugged. 'They will love it.'

'If they want the job they'll accept it.' The Director was blunt. 'But how did they get hold of the crystals in the first place? All operations are external. The shale sifted, the crystals collected, packed into sealed containers, stacked for transportation. It's all done by machines.'

'Machines controlled by men,' reminded Curt. 'The klants need regular maintenance. They come into the station annex to cool — and they bring a few crystals with them.'

'And you claim they are responsible for the deaths of the Venus-returns?' Medway didn't trouble to hide his sneer. 'How can you be so sure? Have you one? Are you dead?'

'No,' said Curt. 'I am not dead but I did have a crystal. I didn't smuggle it back. It was given to me.'

'Impossible!'

'It's the truth. It almost killed me. Would have killed me but for a lucky chance. It slipped into a package of foil I had in my pocket and it stayed there until I found it and gave it to Fenshaw just before he died. It is my belief he was murdered. Someone put that crystal in my pocket when I was here last. It could only have been one of you. Who was it?'

He stared at the startled face of the Director, then at Medway and felt his anger rising.

'Damn you, answer me! Which of you

put that thing into my pocket when we struggled at the edge of the elevator shaft? Who wanted me dead?'

'You must be insane,' snapped Medway. 'Why on earth should I do a thing like that?'

'Did I say it was you?'

Carter said, thickly, 'Are you saying I did it?'

'Is there anyone else?' Curt stared at the Director. 'In your position you would have no trouble at all in getting hold of a crystal. You should know their potential. The ability they have to alter the probability factor. To turn the highly improbable into the extremely likely?'

'No,' said Carter. 'I didn't know that. I never even suspected it. Even if I had you surely don't hold me responsible for the deaths of those men?'

'No,' admitted Curt. 'I don't think that. There's no logic to it. You'd have no motive and nothing to gain. But if it wasn't you then it could only have been one other.' He stared at Medway. 'There is no one else it could be.'

For a long moment there was silence

then Medway shook his head in undisguised incredulity.

'It seems your recent experiences have affected your mind, Harris. Just what are you accusing me of? That I, a person of some reputation, would deliberately attempt to arrange your murder? Why should I do that? What motive would I have? I have less to gain than the Director and yet you have absolved him of blame. I fail to understand your logic.'

'He has a point,' said Carter. 'He's been with the Corporation almost as long as I have. He's worked with the tri-polar crystals all along. In fact I'd say he is the foremost expert on them. You just can't accuse him as you have.'

'I can and I do,' said Curt. 'Only you and he were with me at the elevator shaft. One of you planted that crystal on me. If it wasn't you then it has to be Medway.'

'I didn't do it.'

'That I accept. So we know who did. I want to know why.'

Medway said, 'If you persist in playing this childish game I desire to leave. There is no point in my staying.' Rising from his chair he added, 'If you feel that I am no longer to be trusted, Director, you had best terminate my contract.'

'No,' said Carter. 'Wait!'

'To listen to further insults and insane accusations? Harris is the one who should provide the explanations. What if he had the crystal from the beginning? Smuggled it back from Venus as he claims all the others did. What if he intended to plant it on you? If he really believes it is dangerous what better way to dispose of it? To arrange the later suicide of the Director of the IDC. What would happen to the value of the shares in such an event? Those with advance knowledge would make fortunes. You want a motive? I've just given you one.'

A motive Carter could understand.

'Is there any truth in what he's just said, Harris?'

'No.'

'But he makes a point. We've only your word you didn't smuggle back a crystal. It could be as Medway suggests and that, for some reason, you are — ' He broke off as the intercom hummed its signal. 'Yes?'

He listened to the brief message. 'Right. Send it in.'

It was the crystal Curt had found in the foil packet. The one he had given to Fenshaw and which he firmly believed had caused the man's death. Security had delivered it in a small box, now opened, the object glowing in the sunlight illuminating the windows.

A fragment of Venus. Beautiful, strange, alien.

Curt looked at it then at the other two men. Carter registered no emotion but Medway seemed to have difficulty in breathing. He stood tense beside his chair, one hand grasping the back for support.

'An odd thing, isn't it?' said Curt. 'I guess neither of you have been to Venus but you must know all about the conditions there. Know, too, that incredible as it may seem, actual life has been discovered among the searing rocks and lava, the savage, volcanic heat.'

'Two kinds,' said Carter. 'We know.'

'A small, flat worm-like thing,' said Curt. 'Together with what seems to be a leaf but isn't. They shouldn't survive but they do. Not surprising, really, we have similar contradictions on our own world. Deep in our oceans, near spouting fumaroles of volcanic activity, living organisms thrive in seemingly impossible habitats. We have living creatures in the arctic regions and, everywhere, we have bacteria and viruses that seem able to survive in an extreme range of temperatures.'

Medway said, impatiently, 'Must we listen to this lecture? We are aware there are two types of primitive life on Venus — what of it?'

'Not two,' said Curt. 'Three.'

'What?' The Director shook his head. 'Two, Harris. Not three.'

'Three,' insisted Curt. 'My guess is we could even find more given the time and equipment to investigate. For now we have the worms, the leaves — and the crystals.' Reaching out he shook the small box and moved the one it contained. 'An alien life-form,' he said. 'From Venus.'

'Ridiculous!' Medway was quick with his objection. 'A crystal isn't alive. No more than a diamond is alive. They are both formed in the same way — by the application of intense heat and pressure.'

'So everyone seems to think. But they aren't the same. A diamond is crystallized carbon. This,' he shook the box again, 'has an entirely different composition. One far more complicated and of far greater use. Diamonds look pretty and can cut glass. Tri-polar crystals can open the doors which will yield us the universe.'

Carter had yet to be convinced.

'Life? I think you're going too far, Harris. If they were sentient we would know it.'

'How? Why? We gather them as if they were fish in an ocean. Limpets scraped off rocks. We know fish are alive because they move and eat and breed. Limpets are a little different. They don't seem to move but we know they are alive because they multiply. As do bacteria and viruses. As do the tri-polar crystals.' Curt gestured to the one on the desk. 'We harvest them. The Station restricts our field of operations and the klants can only go so far. Yet we have no trouble in finding the crystals. Where do the replacements come from? If they didn't multiply production would be falling. The Station would have to be moved.'

'An odd conclusion.' said Medway. 'Together with a most peculiar line of reasoning. Surely, Director, you cannot take this man seriously?'

Curt said, flatly, 'Why did you put the crystal in my pocket?'

'I have already denied doing so.'

'Which proves to me you are a liar.' Curt drew in his breath and forced himself to master his anger. 'If the Director hadn't given me his packet of medicinal tablets your action would have led to my death. By sheer luck I put them in the pocket holding the crystal. I was careless in closing the packet and, somehow, the crystal got inside. The foil must have dampened its influence. I was fortunate. When free of the dampening influence it regained its full power. That's why Fenshaw died. That's why I say, without any shadow of doubt, that you murdered him.'

'Nonsense!'

'This is getting us nowhere.' Carter was impatient. 'You made an accusation, Harris, and Medway denies it. He has no evidence that he is innocent but he doesn't need it. You have to supply the proof that he is guilty. As yet you haven't done that.'

'The crystal — '

'Is just that — a crystal. You make it sound as if it's a bomb. You even hint that it could be alive which is obviously ridiculous. I'm sorry, Harris, but I've known and worked with Medway for years. I have to give him the benefit of the doubt.' He reached for the intercom. 'I'll summon security and have them escort you from the building.'

'A moment.' Curt picked up the crystal and rolled it in his palm. 'Just a crystal, you say. Harmless. You agree, Medway?'

'Of course.'

'Then you won't mind carrying it, will you?'

'What? I . . . ' Medway backed as Curt moved towards him, his voice rising in a shriek of protest. 'No!'

'Here. Take it.'

'No! I don't want it! Director, help me!'

'Harris! What the hell are you doing?'

Curt ignored the question as he reached Medway. Anger and frustration added to his strength and the man crumpled in his grasp. Deliberately he plunged his hand into the man's jacket and thrust the crystal hard into an inner pocket where it penetrated the lining.

'Don't touch it,' he warned. 'Just leave it there.'

'I can't! I won't!'

'Think again!' Curt turned to Carter. 'Get security in here. Make sure they don't let Medway remove the crystal.' As the Director hesitated he snapped, 'What's the problem? The thing is harmless. You heard him swear to it. If it is he has nothing to worry about.' To Medway he said, 'Just relax. Take a seat. Maybe we won't need security just some refreshments. Wine, perhaps, or some coffee or tea.'

'Go to hell!'

'I've been there. They call it Venus.'

'You should have died!'

'I did that too, remember?' Curt added, 'Did you report that to the Oracle? Did it make any difference to your own prediction of death?' He saw Medway's expression and, suddenly, everything became clear. 'It did! That's why you want to get rid of the crystal! You fool! Why did you do it? What the hell do you hope to gain?'

Carter said, 'What are you talking about. Do you want security or not?'

'No,' said Curt. 'Not now. They aren't necessary. The less who know about this the better.'

'Know about what?'

'Tell him,' said Medway. 'You might as well. You have probably guessed it all by now and you might as well have the credit for what it's worth.'

He stepped back, his hands visible at his sides as he turned and headed towards the windows. Sunlight illuminated his features and brightened his hair as he stared at the scene outside. The clouds and blue expanse of the sky. The drifting monitors with their twinkling scanners.

The buildings, the city, the people like ants moving far below.

'I'm dying. A wasting disease for which nothing can be done. You might have guessed it — no strength, poor physique, all the rest of it. I've tried but nothing seems to help. I just haven't the energy to continue. Not that it matters. Not now.'

'The Oracle?'

'Yes. No one could work with it as I have and not be curious. I simply had to know.'

'How long?' Curt shouted as he saw what Medway intended. 'Don't! Don't do it! Carter, grab him!'

It was too late. Before either of them could reach him Medway had vanished, diving through a window, which swung open at his touch, the pane unaccountably unfastened. An accident that should never have happened.

On the floor a scrap of paper fluttered in the sudden breeze.

Curt picked it up and read aloud what it said. 'Prediction. Probability that the subject will terminate within twelve hours. 99.99. Within nine hours. 99.99.

231

Within six hours. 99.99.'

'Medway,' said Carter. 'That's why he jumped. But I still can't see what the crystals have to do with it.'

'I told you — they change the order of probability. Medway knew that and a lot more.' Curt shivered as if at a touch of chill, a feeling that once had been described as someone walking on his grave. 'To hell with it. I need a drink.'

A twin of the receptionist supplied it, delivering the bottle and glasses at the Director's summons. She smiled, poured and vanished. As the dead body below had vanished, but memories were harder to dispose of.

The brandy helped and Curt savoured it, inhaling its fragrance, sipping it, feeling its warmth then, in a silent toast, emptying the glass in a single swallow.

'Things aren't always what they seem,' he said as the Director refilled his glass. 'Even on Earth we are deluded by various life-forms and ignorant about the abilities of many more. How could we be so conceited as to think we could cope with a truly alien life form? Medway must have

232

guessed the truth when he built the cybernetic machine. It is a complex mesh of tri-polar crystals able to, in a sense, read the contents of a human brain. Certainly able to take all available data and extrapolate from it and deliver predictions on the probability of selected events. We'll never know just when he discovered the crystals were sentient.'

Carter choked over his brandy. 'Alive? But — '

'We know nothing about them but Medway learned what they could do and how to make them do it. His main object was to maintain a cloak of secrecy. His second to command the Station. Kill all the workers returning from Venus and you know what trouble you'd be in. He used the crystals to do it.'

'Clever.' Carter sipped at his brandy. 'But he's dead now and it's over.'

'You think so?' Curt sat, thinking, remembering how Medway had looked. A man, dying, running out of time — or a man who had served his purpose?

'How close are you to launching the Oracle?' Then as the Director hesitated.

'Let me put it another way. Could you launch it if you wanted?'

'Yes.'

'If the Station ceased production how long could you make do with the crystals you have?'

'Not too long,' said Carter. 'Even though most of the essential installations are complete we need to maintain the supply for further expansion. Why do you ask? The problem's solved. We'll have no more trouble.'

'There will always be trouble,' said Curt. 'There always has been. Each time one culture meets another there is conflict. It's inevitable.'

'What are you getting at?'

'We've contacted an alien race,' said Curt. 'One we've incorporated into most of our essential installations. With the Oracle you have given it the means and opportunity to read our minds and learn everything we know. If it came to a conflict who would you say would win?'

Carter said nothing, but poured himself more brandy.

'The crystals are sentient and can

communicate with each other. Those in the Oracle triggered off those like the one Medway gave to me. I'll even guess they come to be collected at the Station. Why not? They are planet-bound and we supply a means of transport. We thought we were using them but, all along, they have been using us. We can't even guess what their purpose is. The only thing we can be sure of is that we are in a hell of a situation.'

Curt lifted his glass.

'I drink to the future,' he said. 'To mankind getting some common sense. To the hope we can learn from history. We are facing an inevitable conflict — God grant we survive it!'

THE END

FIFTY DAYS TO DOOM
THE DEATH ZONE
THE STELLAR LEGION
STARDEATH
TOYMAN
STARSLAVE
S.T.A.R. FLIGHT
TO DREAM AGAIN
THE WAGER

We do hope that you have enjoyed reading this large print book.

Did you know that all of our titles are available for purchase?

We publish a wide range of high quality large print books including:
Romances, Mysteries, Classics
General Fiction
Non Fiction and Westerns

Special interest titles available in large print are:
The Little Oxford Dictionary
Music Book, Song Book
Hymn Book, Service Book

Also available from us courtesy of Oxford University Press:
Young Readers' Dictionary
(large print edition)
Young Readers' Thesaurus
(large print edition)

For further information or a free brochure, please contact us at:
Ulverscroft Large Print Books Ltd.,
The Green, Bradgate Road, Anstey,
Leicester, LE7 7FU, England.
Tel: (00 44) **0116 236 4325**
Fax: (00 44) **0116 234 0205**

Other titles in the
Linford Mystery Library:

RENEGADE LEGIONNAIRE

Gordon Landsborough

General Sturmer, formerly a Nazi officer in the German desert forces, now leads a group of renegade Arab headhunters, tracking down Foreign Legion deserters — a lucrative business. Meanwhile, ex-cowboy Legionnaire Texas is planning revenge. He aims to capture Sturmer and bring him to face justice in America for his war crimes. In Tunisia, during the war, Sturmer had been responsible for the deaths of thousands of prisoners . . . and one of them had been Tex's brother . . .

DEVIL'S PLAGUE

Michael R. Collings

On a summer's morning, a young woman's body lay battered and broken at the bottom of Porcupine Falls. Who was responsible? Was it the local boy, who was so enamoured with her? Or the stranger with the hidden past? And what is the role of the Devil's Plague? It is up to Lynn Hanson and her friend, Victoria Sears, to examine the clues left by the killer and explain the mystery of the death at Porcupine Falls.

CASEY CLUNES INVESTIGATES

Geraldine Ryan

A pregnant Casey Clunes investigates a case of baby snatching. Young Gemma Stebbings' baby has disappeared from the nursery at Brockhaven Hospital. But all the CCTV footage of medical staff and visitors reveals nothing — so where is baby Justin, and who is responsible? *In at the Deep End* finds Casey attending a reception for a Cambridge college's new swimming pool at Doughty Hall. Author Susannah Storey performs the opening ceremony . . . then her dead body is discovered, floating in the pool . . .

THE CRIMSON RAMBLERS

Gerald Verner

Ready to perform in Andy McKay's concert party on the pier pavilion at Westpool, *The Crimson Ramblers* face more than they imagine . . . As they travel by train to Westpool and enter a dark tunnel, a mysterious packet is thrown into their compartment. Then their summer show becomes a focal point for murder, mystery and sudden death. There are many people anxious to get possession of the packet — who are they? And why are ready to commit murder for it?